# SHORT S

# VOLU

# (2017-2018)

## MATTHEW E. POINTON

# Contents

Dancing the Rasa Lila     4

Conversations over Coffee     20

By the Water's Edge     26

The Sage in Staffordshire     32

Piece of My Heart     40

Caféncounters     43

The Sun of the Nation 男     53

The Sun of the Nation 女     60

Laying the Foundations of the New Albania     65

Confirmed by History     70

Wanna Play?     79

Dance Me to the End of Love     87

St. Pancras     91

Victoria Falls     96

Day Off     101

No New Messages, No Missed Calls     108

Death in Paradise     112

Victory     125

Three Strangers     147

Hole in the Soul     154

Unto China     173

Alto de Perdón     218

Lost & Found                                      222

Callous Caller on the 08:25                       227

# Dancing the Rasa Lila

*'But Lord Krishna knew the hearts of the Gopis. He turned the hearts of the Gopis to the proper direction by completely eradicating lust from their minds. It is with this purpose in view that Lord Krishna played the Rasa Lila with the Gopis. At the time of Rasa Lila, He multiplied Himself into so many Krishnas. The Gopis were struck with wonder and amazement. All their idea of physical love entirely vanished due to this miracle. They witnessed the showers of flowers poured from the skies by the Devas. They saw the Vidyadharas, Gandharvas, Yakshas, Charanas, etc., singing the praise of the Lord. They enjoyed the blissful company of the Lord at the time of Rasa Lila, a bliss millions of times greater than the bliss they would enjoy through sense objects. They enjoyed the bliss of Samadhi or union with God.'*[1]

*'Among all the gopis in Vrindavan, Radha was Krishna's favourite. She was the daughter of a cowherd Vrishabhanu and Kamalavati of Barsana. Radha loved Krishna deeply and was very devoted to him.'*[2]

# Act I

You ask me of love.

An old man who is single and content to be that way, what would he know of love? But I do know. Oh yes, I know all too well.

I remember it as if it were yesterday even though over three score years have passed between that day and this. I recall it with absolute crystal

---

[1] http://www.kirtimukha.com/surfings/SriKrishna/krishnalilas/krishnalilas10.htm

[2] http://www.kidsgen.com/fables_and_fairytales/indian_mythology_stories/radha.htm

clarity even though I struggle to remember what I ate for breakfast this morning.

It was in the April of 1997 and it was a Friday. I was on my year out from university and volunteering on a kibbutz in Israel, busy turning the desert green. All us volunteers were in the coffee shop where we socialised after a day in the fields when in walked a group of people whom we had not seen before. They were the new batch of Ulpan students, recent Jewish émigrés from the Soviet Union who were learning Hebrew before embarking upon their new lives in the Promised Land.

She took my breath away. She had olive brown skin, dark eyes of melted chocolate and lustrous black tresses. This was Israel and the Queen of Sheba had arrived.

I later learnt that her name was Rada.

O Rada!

Over the weeks that followed I got to know her for she was posted to work in the same team as me in the olive groves. She was Russian by passport but Soviet was a far better description for she was truly a product of that dead empire. Her father hailed from Tartarstan whilst he mother was Armenian and she had grown up in Leningrad, a city no longer on the map. She belonged to nowhere and everywhere but to me she seemed most at home there, playing with me in the olive groves.

O Rada!

She was there as an immigrant with her husband of but one year. His name was Andrei and his Jewish grandmother had qualified both of them for Israeli citizenship. She'd given up her degree to be with him. "What did you study?" I'd asked her. "BA Study of Religions," she'd replied. I couldn't believe it; the same as me! We shared a passion!

O Rada!

Around the campfire in the long desert evenings she would talk for hours about that passion. She was so excited to be in Israel, the land where so many religions began, although her heart was not in Judaism. She did not profess to a particular creed herself; her father's family had been nominally Muslim; her mother, like all Armenians, Christian, and her upbringing, firmly atheist. But she had a fascination with the Eastern faiths and would wax lyrical about Krishna and Radha. I had just completed a module on the Hare Krishna Movement and wondered if she had, perhaps, not been a member, since they were growing exponentially in Russia at that time. She would joke that our names were almost identical to those of the famous lovers and I would get out my guitar and play Kula Shaker songs which she would clap and sing along to and for a while it seemed almost as if the kibbutz was transformed into the forest groves of Vrindavan, that the other volunteers and the Ulpan students were the gopis and that...

...and then the illusion was shattered when Andrei would come up to his wife, kiss her on the neck and suggest that they turn in for the night.

O Rada!

After I left Israel to return to my studies in England, we kept in touch, Rada and I, by letter. Her missives were long and poetical, full of the joys of life. She included photographs with them which I pinned to my wall, guiltily covering up Andrei by accident with a postcard from a friend in New Zealand, the icon thus becoming a focus for my devotions.

I'd gaze at her image, the spring-bodied Rada whose limbs are made of the beauty of flowers of the madhavi creeper and, in the intensity of my love, I would whisper her name like a mantra, "Rada, Radha, Rada!"

O Rada!

But then, after Christmas, the letters ceased and I knew that something had happened. The months passed in agonising silence and my Beloved's pain I felt in my breast. I knew that I had to see her, to be with her and so, when the Easter holidays came, that great time of renewal and hope, I boarded a plane to Tel Aviv and I travelled over the lands and seas silently calling out her name.

O Rada!

She was not in the kibbutz as I knew she wouldn't be. Friends told me that she and Andrei had separated acrimoniously and that she now slept on the sofa at the home of Tanya, another friend from the kibbutz. They provided me with the address and I found it easily, a drab apartment on the fringes of Tel Aviv, Israel's drabbest city. Summoning up my courage, I went to the door and rang the bell. There was silence for some seconds and then it opened and there she stood, my lotus-faced, subtle-bodied Beloved, her beautiful black eyes alive at the sight of my arriving.

O Rada!

That night we talked and we laughed and we sang. Joy and love flowed within those walls but it was not the same as it had been before. In such a place it never could be and with great sadness I knew that it was not to be. The time had passed... unless...

"What are your plans?" asked Tanya.

"I must leave here," I replied. "I have to go to Jerusalem."

"The Holy City," said Rada.

"Would you like to join me?" I asked.

"I cannot," she replied.

"Why not?" I asked.

"I have work and I have appointments and things to do and..."

I longed to tell her that these things did not matter, that they were but illusions, that only love matters...

...but my courage failed me and I did not.

O Rada!

# Act II

I never expected you. When you rang the bell of that drab apartment in that drab city. When my life was at its lowest, I never expected you to call.

But there you were, standing on my doorstep, entering my life at its lowest ebb just as you had at its highest.

With a smile.

And your guitar slung across your back.

---

You knew. Even though I had gone out of my way not to tell you, you knew. It was as if you'd sensed it, the pain in my heart, the shame, the despair. From a thousand miles away you'd shared it and you'd journeyed over land and sea to be with me. To be there at my side. As in the Govinda Gita, I had called...

O Krishna!

...and you had answered.

O Radha!

But was it right? Surely not! Surely you should not have come!

---

They were the happiest of times.

They were the carefree times of youth, sandwiched in-between the abrasive realities of adult life. I still cherish those memories even though they feel over half a lifetime away.

And yet they were but a single year in the past.

When we arrived on the kibbutz, Andrei and I were still in love. Or at least, we believed ourselves to be. In all honesty though, how can one fully understand the workings of the human heart at such a tender age?

But then can one ever fully understand the workings of the human heart at any age?

Later, after we had parted with such acrimony and the tongues had begun to wag, their words pierced me like arrows. Even today I nurse the wounds that they caused.

*She used him! I feel for the man; he was taken advantage of!*

*She's nothing but a whore! I heard she went with half the men here!*

*She only married him for the passport you know!*

*Nothing but a gold-digger and a user!*

*So what if she is in tears? The bitch deserves everything that she's got!*

But do I deserve all those tears and wounds? Did I use him for my only ends, only to cast him aside when my goal was won?

I don't know, Lord, I truly do not know!

I did love him... I think. I was attracted to he, that much I do know, and he to me. Surely that is enough?

Isn't it?

But I must confess that another dream blazed just as brightly as love across the constellations of my heart: the dream of a new life; a dream of hope; a dream of escape from that drab world of no opportunities.

Yet here I am now, sitting in another drab world with no opportunities laid before me.

Perhaps it was not Andrei whom I married but Maya.

Yes indeed, it *was* Maya. For when we were alone, when the suffocating quilts of familiarity and normality had been draped over our inert bodies, then that which I had loved about him disappeared and in its place...

...

O Maya, I wish you well, but you shall never be a mate for me!

But back then Maya had not made his... her... their... true nature known and it was as if we were in a forest by the Yamuna rather than a desert near the Jordan. We were young, we were happy, we were carefree. We had escaped! Only joy lay before us! We had a whole new world to discover!

And then you arrived.

I saw you standing there, just as you were a year later when you rang my bell, the curls of your hair falling on your temple, your guitar slung across your back and a smile on your face.

And at that moment I learned what devotion is.

Devotion. Is that the right word? I could have said "love" for love it was... is... but if I say "love" then they won't understand.

Not that they could ever understand anyway.

No one can who has not danced the rasa lila with you.

For this love, this devotion, was not like love in the sense commonly accepted by this shallow world. I was not thinking of betraying my husband for you, nor would I have thought in such a way even if I were not married. No, it was different indeed. Instead, when we sat around that campfire and you told me that you were studying the same things that I had studied, that your interests and passions mirrored my own so completely, that you understood all about Radha, Krishna, the gopis and the Yamuna, then it was as if we were not two people but instead two halves of the same whole just waiting to be put back together.

And when you took out your guitar – Oh why could it not have been a flute?! – and I lost myself in your song, then the desert became a forest, the other students and volunteers the gopis, you Krishna as your names hints and I, well, I became true to my name also.

    And Maya?

    Oh Maya was truly absent on those perfect evenings!

---

But in that drab apartment in that drab town a year later when Maya's true nature had revealed itself and the glorious facade of my new life had crumbled to dust so that only an absence of hope remained; in there, that vale of sorrows, even your smile and song could not conjure up the forest.

I asked you what you would be doing and you replied that you would visit Jerusalem.

    The City of Peace.

    The Holy City.

You had come but now you were leaving again. It was too cruel.

"Come with me!" you urged.

But I refused, citing a thousand examples of Maya as my excuses.

That night though, in the dark, as we shared a bed so as to give you the sofa, my dear friend Tanya and I spoke.

"You are thinking of him."

"Not in that way."

"Did I say in that way?"

"No, but you thought it."

"I did not. I can see that what there is between you two is different. Perhaps he is like a brother to you, not a lover."

"You are wrong. He is my lover, but just not in that way."

"If that is so, then why do you not go to him?"

"What do you mean?"

"He calls you, 'O Rada!' I can hear his voice."

"And I am to reply, 'O Chris, here I am!' I suppose?"

"If that is your desire."

"I cannot."

"You can. You must."

"I cannot. I have work. I have things to sort out, places I need to be..."

"Go! I will lead you!"

"It is not possible."

"It is essential; go!"

And so, the next morning, I travelled with you to the Holy City.

---

Do you remember that bus journey? How I laid my head on your shoulder and watched this sad world of Maya pass us by as we travelled from the secular to the sacred? I remember it and I treasure those memories with bliss. How you ran your fingers through my hair. You did not ask how I was feeling or what I was thinking for you already knew. All you said was, "There is no shame in your actions, Rada, whatever people might say. You have let no one down."

---

There was some trouble getting a room I seem to recall, although the details of how we resolved it are lost to me now. They are irrelevant anyway. But every precious second of us walking through the City of Peace hand-in-hand, joined as one, now that is engraved upon my heart forever. And then we sat before the Kotel.

Ahh yes, the Kotel.

O Chris!

O Krishna!

What happened there before the Kotel?

That question is one that I cannot truly answer.

We sat there, on a bench, that holiest of places before us, our hands entwined like two vines, and something happened.

Something beyond all else that I have ever experienced.

It was the holiness of the place I suppose, the effect of all those countless millions of prayers lodged between the stones for God to read.

Even though we were motionless, the blood pulsed through our body.

Yes, I said "our body" in the singular, for we were as one.

And even though we didn't move a muscle, inside we were alive and dancing.

Dancing the rasa lila.

I heard his flute and it ravished my soul.

The little golden bells on the girdle around my waist chimed with joy.

And the jewelled bangles on my wrists made music as they shook.

And my silver anklets tinkled with ecstatic union.

Spring came laden with flowers as the unbidden, uncontrolled rapture of youth!

My ample thighs and love-filled breasts went to him.

And he whispered,

"O Radha, be Me!"

And I was.

We were one.

And the sweet smells of clove and sandal filled the air.

I touched his hand and we rose without a word.

---

That night I dreamt the sweetest of dreams, but I shall not relate them here.

---

In the morning I awoke before him as I knew I must. I sat watching his sleeping form, his chest rising and falling, and I wished it could be forever.

But just as Radha had to marry Abhimanyu and live her life without Krishna, so too does Rada.

And just as Krishna had to leave Vrindavan to fight the Kurukshetra War, so too does Chris.

I wrote him a note and then, with a tear of amber nectar in my eye, I kissed my beloved on the forehead and slipped away.

# Act III

The next morning when I arose, Tanya had left for work but Rada was still there. She had cooked me breakfast and the scents of her labours filled the rooms. As she served it she said simply, "I shall accompany you to Jerusalem."

O Rada!

When we arrived there old tales were written anew. Due to the Easter celebrations all the hotels and hostels were booked-up full. We wandered from place to place but there was no room at any inn. Fearful that we would have to return to Tel Aviv unfulfilled, we stepped into the last place listed in the guidebook.

"I have only one room left but I cannot give it to you," said the innkeeper. "It is a double room and we only let our double rooms to married couples."

"But I am married!" protested my Beloved, showing her ring as proof.

"But the names on your passports are different."

"That is because I did not change mine when I married. That is common in Russia. But look, it clearly says that 'Mrs' and not 'Miss'."

And so he relented and we received the last room. When we were alone inside it I said "Was that honest?" to which she replied, "Yes, of course. I lied neither legally nor spiritually, for he never asked to whom I was married and, in our hearts, I believe that we have a union far greater than that which any legal document can bestow."

I could not disagree.

O Rada!

We wandered around the Old City which I remembered in parts from my visit there the year before. I took her to the Armenian Quarter where she joked she might have relatives and we prayed at both Calvary and the Empty Tomb. But, as the sun was setting, we ended up at the Kotel, the former Western Wall of the great temple built by Herod to house the Holiest of Holies.

Even more than the rest of that day of days, I remember this as clearly as if it happened only seconds ago. Indeed, even as I speak to you now, I can see it with my eyes – the dying sun is bleaching the creamy stones pink, the air is fragrant with warmth and spices and the shampoo of her hair which rests on my shoulder. We sit down on a bench overlooking the plaza, lace our fingers together and watch the hundreds of worshippers praying at that holiest of shrines, their heads nodding in supplication to the God who is, according to the His six-pointed star, both male and female combined. The very air is thick with prayer and it is so powerful. We do not speak, we cannot; it would be profane to break that most sacred silence. We are lost in awe and wonder. There in that place and yet, somehow, somewhere else too. And we are we no longer, but instead only I. Never before have I known such a feeling, such total communion with another soul; the feeling of ecstasy and union within me rises up to erupt like a volcano. This truly is the rasa lila.

O Beloved, melt into me and overflow above all barriers into me.

O Rada, be me!

How long we sat there I cannot say, but it the sky was dark when she wordlessly put her arm around my waist and we rose to return to the hotel.

And that night, O Rada, I dreamt.

---

I was in a pleasure garden in a forest with flower bowers and other trysting nooks. The blossoms of spring were all around. There were cattle to be seen and, tending those most gentle of beasts, the beautiful gopis. I sat on a rock, got out my guitar and started to play and the gopis, hearing my song, forgot their tasks and made their way towards me. I started to play faster, a more joyful melody and the gopis began to clap their hands, rattle their bangles and anklets and dance, circling around and around, their colourful dresses merging with the forest flowers. And they started to sing also and gestured for me to join them and so I stopped my playing but the music continued regardless, only increasing in its beauty. And I went up with them, linked hands with them and started spinning around surrounded by joyful, laughing faces, swirling golds, greens, pinks and blues and the sound of singing and happiness and I became lost, lost in a trance of ecstasy and love, lost in the rasa lila, that exquisite dance of the spirit.

And then I felt one pair of hands take mine and lead me away from the group. And I let her lead me at first but then I felt a tinge of guilt – or was it sadness – towards the other gopis and so, like Lot's wife, I glanced back at them and, to my shock and amazement, I saw that I had not left but that I was still there, multiplied a hundred time so that each and every gopi danced with me alone, each lost in their own personal rasa lila.

But you and I, instead we made our way down the green pathways through the forest until we came to a river of crystal waters. And there You looked Me in the eyes, Your face transfigured into the goddess that You are, and said, "My soul was in torment, separated from You; O Krishna, You make me alive again!"

17

And there, by the waters of the Yamuna, our lips met and You dissolved into Me with flashes of lightning.

O Radha!

---

The following morning I awoke and she... You... were gone. What had happened? Where were You? And the dream; it had been so powerful, so real...

Then I saw the letter that You had left.

*Chris,*

*When we first met we joked about our names. I always knew that they were more than mere coincidence.*

*Radha went out into the moonlight,*
*in the light of the white soft moon,*
*white everywhere,*
*wearing a white robe to meet her Lord.*
*So she concealed herself in the white*
*and roamed as the light itself in search of Him.*

*Love eternally,*

*Rad(h)a*

I cried when I read that letter and I cried on the bus back to Tel Aviv. But after that I did not cry again.

Instead I thanked God for the rasa lila that we danced together.

And even after I married and started a family of my own, I always remembered You and kept a flame burning for You in my heart.

And now that such earthly cares have passed away and we stand by the banks of the Yamuna again, why not dance with me once more

O Beloved

O Rada

O Radha.

*Written January 2017, Smallthorne, UK*

# Conversations over Coffee

## 14:00 Outside Patisserie Valerie on Great Cumberland Place

Simon was walking to his appointment when he saw her. Swathed all in black, even the eyes, more a mound of material than a human being. He was not prejudiced, racist, certainly not an Islamophobe, but that really was too much. How could she live like that? So separated from the rest of the world. Even her hand that held the coffee cup was gloved. Open-minded and liberal thought he might be, *that* was wrong.

"Can I help you?"

"Excuse me?"

"You were staring at me. Is something up?"

Her voice, slightly muffled by her veil, had the unmistakable accent of a British Asian. He wasn't surprised: our home-grown Muslims are often far more fanatical than the imported ones. That's why he'd never had an issue with Syrian immigrants. Just look at the 7/7 bombers...

"I wasn't staring at you."

"Yes you were, very clearly. Is there something that I can help you with?"

He felt awkward; he didn't need this, certainly not now. He glanced at his watch. Only an hour away...

"No, no, I'm sorry, I..."

"No, come, please, have a coffee with me. My shout." She motioned with her gloved hands to the waiter. "How do you take it?"

"Well, I..."

Simon was torn. This was all incredibly embarrassing but at the same time he wanted to talk to this veiled phantom. He had stared at her and he did want to know what it was like to live in such a way. And here was his chance. But the appointment, he had to be ready, on top of his game..."

"Well what?"

"Well the thing is, I have an appointment at three and I..."

"Which gives you an hour to drink a single cup of coffee. Plenty of time. Don't be scared; I've not got a bomb hidden under here you know."

"No, I never imagined... yes, alright then, I shall... and thanks, for the coffee I mean. It's very kind of you."

"It's nothing," she replied. "Shamira Begum by the way. I'd shake your hand but we're not meant to have contact like that with unrelated men."

"But talking is ok?"

"Sure it is. So long as we do not deliberately make our voices sound provocative or sexy. It's all about the modesty see. You don't find my voice too sexy I hope."

"No, not at all... I mean, well, it is a nice voice, but... I..."

"Simon, I was joking. Sit down and tell me what you want."

The coffees came. Simon sipped his. Shamira skilfully lifted her veil from the side and sipped hers too. Not an inch of her skin was revealed.

"My name's Simon by the way, Simon O'Neill. And yes, I did stare. I'm sorry, I shouldn't have but, well... I've always wondered what it must be like to live and dress like you do."

"Lots of people wonder about it, but thanks for your honesty and maybe I can satisfy that curiosity. But for starters, my husband doesn't force me to wear the veil, before you ask. In fact, I'm not even married. It is my choice."

"I never imagined that he did. That stereotype might have rung true once upon a time but today I guess it is more of a choice based on religious convictions."

"And lifestyle choice. I dress like this because I find it liberating. People don't judge me on how I appear: my race, looks and so on. Dressed like this, they have to engage with the real me."

"I appreciate that, but how can it be liberating? I mean, aren't you hot under all those layers and the gloves and even your eyes are hidden. How can you see clearly? Surely it must be difficult.

"Not really. I don't usually wear the eyeveils, certainly never while driving or reading. They're only down today necause it's so bright and sunny. It's the same as looking through sunglasses. And as for the rest, whilst they can be warm sometimes, at the same time they're loose so there's a free flow of air. Certainly more comfortable than high heels and skin-tight jeans."

A young lady wearing just those walked past them on the street, talking into her phone. Simon's eyes were immediately drawn to her but he purposefully shifted them back to his coffee companion whose eyes he now realised, he could just about discern behind her veil. He wondered what she looked like. She sounded young but was she eighteen or thirty-eight? And was she beautiful or ugly? She was an enigma... and she wanted to be.

"I'm sorry... about the staring. I know it's rude..."

"Forget it, I get it all the time. People might not be staring at me in a sexual way but whatever you wear; I don't think you can ever cure the curiosity. But anyway, enough about me, what about you Simon O'Neill, tell me about your life?"

If he hadn't been talking to an obviously fundamentalist mound of material, Simon would have sworn that was the start of a chat-up.

"Not much to say. Also single, thirty, work as a journalist..."

"Whoa! Stop right there! A journalist, eh? I think you'd better leave!"

"What do you mean?"

"Well I don't want to be picking up the Sun or the Mirror tomorrow and be reading all about 'My meeting with Shrouded Shamira, a symptom of the Islamic evil sweeping the nation'!"

He laughed though he knew the kind of journalism that she was referring to. "Don't worry, I don't write that kind of thing. No politics for me; my stuff is far more frothy."

"Frothy, eh? Sounds intriguing. So, no stories about Shrouded Shamira, deal?"

"Deal."

---

They relaxed and talked over the rest of their coffee, but when it was drained, Simon stood up and said, "Sorry Shamira, this has been an absolute pleasure, it really has, but, as I said before, I have an interview to conduct at three."

"A big one?"

"My biggest yet. If I do well it could open doors so I really don't want to mess it up."

"Don't worry, you'll be fine. Talk to her as you've talked to me and she'll be putty in your hands..."

## 15:10 Lanes of London Restaurant, Marriott Hotel, Park Lane

Simon's nervousness dissipated the moment Kelly Rettinger stepped into the restaurant late by a full ten minutes. As with the rest of the room – and indeed every room that she ever stepped into – the actress, star of seemingly every blockbuster this year, captivated him. Wearing a plunging cream wrap top (which displayed her famous cleavage to perfection), a curve-hugging charcoal grey maxi skirt (which did the same for her equally famous derriere) and finished off with black high-heels and an elegant black choker, she was the very image of style and sophistication. She was beautiful, incredibly so, even more in the flesh than on the silver screen, and when she flashed her perfect white teeth in a smiled at him and walked over to the table with an intoxicating sway to her gait, he felt himself melt clean away. He stood up, shook her hand and then they kissed, continental-style, cheek-to-cheek, after which she elegantly lowered herself into the chair that he held out for her.

"Are you dining?" he asked.

"No, just a coffee."

---

The interview was going badly, terribly in fact. Before this tour de force of style and sex appeal he floundered and gasped for air like a drowning man. He was blowing it and he knew it. He silently thanked God when her mobile rang and she excused herself to talk to a director a thousand miles away.

As he sat waiting he wondered why it was all going so horribly wrong and his mind cast itself back to the other conversation over coffee that he'd engaged in only an hour earlier. She had been another stranger, captivating in her own way, yet, after his initial nervousness and embarrassment, they had spoken so freely and honestly to each other... and had been so relaxed that it had been pure pleasure, not a chore.

His eyes drifted towards the elegant and manicured fingers of Miss Rettinger who was absent-mindedly playing with her teaspoon as she talked and, in an instant, it hit him: this woman was the exact polar opposite of the other! Whereas she desired to be seen, the other avoided it; whereas she deliberately accentuated the power of her sex appeal, the other purposefully eliminated it and whereas she was all about the externals, the other thought only of what is inside. But what did that mean? And how could he save the interview?

Then the idea struck him: imagine that Kelly Rettinger was Shamira Begum... or at least, dressed like her. He looked across at the starlet and tried to imagine her shrouded completely in black cloth with only her voice for him to base his opinions on. It was hard but it might just work...

---

After Kelly ended her call, the interview changed. Simon relaxed and so did she. They began talking as real human beings, laughing, joking and genuinely enjoying themselves. In fact, behind all the glamour, he discovered that Kelly Rettinger was still the grammar school girl from Grantham who'd got her lucky break. In short, she was good company. She was human.

And when the time came for the interview to end both of them sounded almost disappointed.

And to top it all off, when he'd called for the bill, she had stopped him and said with a smile, "Don't be silly, this is on me. I haven't enjoyed an interview so much in years!"

## 16:30 *Outside Patisserie Valerie on Great Cumberland Place*

Simon knew that Shamira Begum would be long gone from there, but he returned to the scene of their conversation anyway, partially as a tribute to the encounter that had helped make his biggest interview to date such a success. He ordered another coffee, even though he didn't need the caffeine, and started to draft the article. Just as his drink arrived though, his phone pinged.

It was an email and not just any email. It was an email from the personal account of Miss Kelly Rettinger no less! With a feeling of excitement, he opned it.

*Simon,*

*Are you free at 3 tomorrow? I need someone to co-write my autobiography with and I think that you're the man. Meet me at the Patisserie Valerie on Great Cumberland Place if you are interested.*

*Hope you can make it!*

*K xxx*

*P.S. This time though, you're buying the coffee. After all, I paid for the last two* 😉

'Two?' he thought to himself. 'But I only had one!'

Then he realised.

**Written January 5th-6th, 2017, Leek & Hanley, UK**

# By the Water's Edge

*'KRISHNA is GOD, the Source of all that exists, the Cause of all that is, was, or ever will be.*
*As GOD is unlimited HE has many Names.*
*Allah-Buddha-Jehovah-Rama: All are KRISHNA, all are ONE.'*
**George Harrison in 'Kṛṣṇa'**

*'Jesus answered him, "I am the way, the truth, and the life; no one goes to the Father except by me. Now that you have known me," he said to them, "you will know my Father also, and from now on you do know him and you have seen him."'*
**John 14:6-7**

Joshua stepped out of the doorway of his aunt's house and drank in the vista before him.

The waters of the lake twinkled and glittered in the morning sunshine. It was a scene of almost indescribable beauty. He started to mutter a prayer of thanksgiving to the Lord whilst wiping the sleep from his eyes.

> Praise the LORD, my soul!
>     O LORD, my God, how great you are!
> You are clothed with majesty and glory;
>     you cover yourself with light.[3]

Yet even as his tongue tripped over those words of the father, his mind drifted onto some others, those of his son:

> Who is this whose glance is like the dawn?
> She is beautiful and bright,
>     as dazzling as the sun or the moon.
> I have come down among the almond trees
>     to see the young plants in the valley,
>     to see the new leaves on the vines
>     and the blossoms on the pomegranate trees.

---

[3] Psalm 104:1-2

I am trembling; you have made me as eager for love
as a chariot driver is for battle.[4]

"Joshua, come here and drink and eat!"

His aunt's voice snapped him out of his reverie and he smiled.

Yes indeed, what a day for love!

---

First maiden:     Down by the lakeside I saw him, his skin bronzed and smooth.

Second maiden:  Down by the water's edge I glanced at him, sitting on a stone and singing, his hair wavy and black as a raven.

Third maiden:    Down where the waves lap the pebbles, I spied on him as he played his flute, his eyes as beautiful as doves by a flowing brook.

Joshua:           Hiding in amongst the olive trees when they should have been tending their animals, I saw them, the maidens of Magdala, their eyes shining with love, like doves hiding in the crevices of a rock. Oh maidens of Magdala, the loveliest of women!

---

That evening, as the sun was sinking slowly in the sky, Joshua again went down to the water's edge to see the village girls again. As he walked through the olive grove, he heard sounds of splashing and laughter and, hiding behind a tree, he saw that they were bathing in the water and had left their clothes on the beach. Smiling, he made his way down to the water and stole their clothes. Then he revealed himself to the bathers:

"Good evening maidens of Magdala!" he cried with a grin.

---

[4] Song of Solomon 6:10-12

The girls, realising that they were alone, shrieked, "Please sir, leave us here! We cannot be seen naked!"

"Pray tell me, why is that?"

"Nephew of Elisheva, do not joke with us in that way," said Miryam, the loveliest of all the maidens. "Everybody knows that a woman cannot be seen naked before any man except her husband!"

"But did not each and every one of you petition the Lord in your prayers this afternoon to marry me?"

The maidens looked at one another in amazement; how did he know that which had been uttered in private between them and their God? None of them knew what to say.

"So, since you all desired to marry me and since I love you all, then what sin is there in appearing naked before your husband?"

"But how can you claim to be married to us all at the same time?" asked Miryam.

"With the Lord everything is possible," he replied. "And besides, did not King Solomon himself have seven hundred wives?"

And so, seeing that he was determined and they had no alternative but to obey him, one after another they came out of the water, trying to hide their nakedness with their hands and shivering in the evening air. Their simple presentation was so pure that he was immediately pleased with them and as they collected their clothes and began to dress, he sang:

> What a magnificent young woman you are!
>     How beautiful are your feet in sandals.
> The curve of your thighs
>     is like the work of an artist.
> A bowl is there,
>     that never runs out of spiced wine.
> A sheaf of wheat is there,
>     surrounded by lilies.

Your breasts are like twin deer,
   like two gazelles.
Your neck is like a tower of ivory.
Your eyes are like the pools in the city of Heshbon,
   near the gate of that great city.
Your nose is as lovely as the tower of Lebanon
   that stands guard at Damascus.
Your head is held high like Mount Carmel.
Your braided hair shines like the finest satin;
   its beauty could hold a king captive.
How pretty you are, how beautiful;
   how complete the delights of your love.
You are as graceful as a palm tree,
   and your breasts are clusters of dates.
I will climb the palm tree
   and pick its fruit.
To me your breasts are like bunches of grapes,
   your breath like the fragrance of apples,
   and your mouth like the finest wine.[5]

And when he had finished his song and they had all replaced their garments, he took out his flute and started to play and they all retreated into the olive grove singing

Dance, dance, girl of Shulam.
Let us watch you as you dance.[6]

And with those words they began to dance in the grove, swirling around, full of joy and youth, their happiness filling the air. And he danced with them and even though the flute was no longer at his lips, the music kept playing until it engulfed the entire grove and he appeared as a full moon surrounded by shining stars and they all danced with joy, their ecstasy magnifying the beauty of the maidens a hundred-fold.

But there was one maiden whom he loved above all the others, one who was destined to be united with him for all eternity, the one who bore the same name as his mother. He took her by the hand to lead her to the

[5] Song of Solomon 7:1-9
[6] Song of Solomon 6:13

water's edge but then thought of the others, of how unhappy they would be if he left them, and so he prayed to the Lord and lo! As he led his beloved disciple away, he glanced back to see that he had multiplied himself so that each and every maiden was dancing with him and him alone and he smiled for he saw that it was good.

And by the shore of the lake they stood. And he clasped her slender waist and stared into her eyes that shone with love before moving down to her lips like a scarlet ribbon.

He whispered into her ear:

> Women of Zion, come and see King Solomon.
> He is wearing the crown that his mother placed on his head
> on his wedding day,
> on the day of his gladness and joy.[7]

They embraced.

---

Joshua:    How beautiful you are, my love;
        how your eyes shine with love!
Miryam:    How handsome you are, my dearest;
        how you delight me!
    The green grass will be our bed;
        the cedars will be the beams of our house,
        and the cypress trees the ceiling.
    I am only a wild flower in Sharon,
        a lily in a mountain valley.[8]

---

As the sun rose over the crystal sea Miryam looked at Joshua and tears filled her eyes.

"Must you go?" she asked.

---

[7] Song of Solomon 3:11
[8] Song of Solomon 1:15-2:1

"You know that I must," he replied. "I have a mission to fulfil but you shall see me when I return."

She nodded in acceptance of the inevitable. "Please… give me something to remember you by."

"As my kingdom is not of this world, then I can give you no earthly thing," he replied. "But I shall give you this, a new commandment: Love one another as I have loved you."

They recalled the dance and smiled.

"Is that your mission: to love?""

He nodded. "What I have taught you today I shall later teach the whole world."

She smiled and let go of his hand and he slowly walked away.

And tears rolled down her cheeks as the pebbles crunched under his sandals.

*Written 23rd January, 2017, Smallthorne, UK*

# The Sage in Staffordshire

Smoke rose slowly from the candle as Rabindranath sat before it completing his morning puja. As he prayed, his palms together before him, his eyes followed the grey wisps as they curled and looped, sometimes this way and sometimes that, depending on the currents of the air. And as the words of Vedic scripture ran through his head, he meditated that this smoke was like men, being pushed this way or that by an unseen yet omnipotent Creator, regardless of their human wants and desires. 'Which way shall you blow me today?' he asked that Creator silently.

When he rose from his puja though, the rain was beating down heavily on the window. Today at least, he was not to be blown very far.

It rained all that day and the next too, but on the third day when he rose again it had stopped and the sun was shining brightly in the crisp April sky. He could now leave the house which had been as a tomb to him ever since his arrival and, at last, begin to explore this garden which that unseen Creator had blown him into.

And he was eager to do so. Charles had raved about the place on their long journey over. "Oh, you just have to come and stay at the home of my friend Rev. Outram, it is so beautiful, a real gem of a village. The hills thereabouts are splendid for walking and the people, although simple and not well educated, are truly the salt of the earth." Rabin had not needed his good friend's recommendation though; yes, he had enjoyed London and Cambridge very much, the culture and learning that one had access to in those great centres was remarkable, but just as the real Bengal was not to be found in Calcutta, so too it must be that if he wanted to discover real England, to truly understand the culture that had had such an influence over his own, then it was to the small villages among the simple, country folk that he must head.

And whilst it had been a pleasant surprise to discover that Sushil Rudra of St. Stephen College, Delhi and his daughter were also staying at the vicarage, the presence of other Indians meant that most conversations and interactions so far had revolved far more around what he had left that what he had come to experience. But today Sushil and his daughter had left for Manchester along with Charles who had business in that great industrial city and so Rabin was left to his own devices and freed from any associations with his native land.

Taking his stick and putting on a coat to defy the cold English wind, he made his way to the church where his host ministered to the spiritual needs of the populace. It was a graceful building with a slender spire and some fine carvings, but not old, perhaps fifty years at most, although he had been told at dinner the preceding evening that it was built upon much older foundations. That reminded him of so many Hindu temples such as those lining the ghats at Benares: the buildings themselves were quite new but the holiness they embedded was almost timeless. However, that was where the similarities ended for when he opened the door and went inside, what he was struck by – as was always the case when he entered a Christian church – was the silence and the smell. Musty paper mixed with polished wood and brass. It was as different as could be from a Hindu mandir where all was incense, colour and the clanging of gongs and whilst Rabin knew that there are many paths up the mountain to God, and he knew too how Christ had occupied the heart of his friend Charles, he found nothing here. His path was a different one.

Feeling cold and claustrophobic, he went back outside into the sunlight and wandered around the churchyard. The Christian custom of surrounding their temples with the dead had always amused him slightly, but he rather liked this cemetery as many of the graves had poems carved onto the headstones which appealed to the artist in him. He stopped before one and read it.

*Elizabeth Horobin who had died on January the 27th, A.D.*
*1780 aged 73 years.*

*With deepest Thoughts Spectator View thy fate*
*This Mortal path to an immortal fate*
*Through Death's dark Vale we hope she found the Way*
*To the bright Regions of eternal Day*
*Life's but a Moment, Death that Moment ends*
*Thrice happy she is her Moment wisely spends*
*For on that dirful point Eternity depends*

As a poet he had to admit that the quality of the verse – and the standard of punctuation! – was pretty poor but nonetheless it did have a certain power to it. What must it be like, he wondered, to die and then endure an eternity in a place decided by one's sins as the Christians and Muslims believed? He couldn't imagine it; he would die and be reincarnated in another form and that was that, but what of this mysterious Elizabeth Horobin whose remains lay beneath his feet; where was she right now?

He left the churchyard and descended down the hill into the village itself. It was definitely a pretty place, a world away from the flat villages of Bengal, with a main street so steep that he was scared of slipping whilst tiny stone cottages clung to the roadside. The villagers that saw him gazed at him suspiciously, just as a Bengal Brahmin might view a Dalit and it made him chuckle inwardly that he, so noble and high-born, was now the Untouchable. Of course, everyone was aware that the Rector had a mysterious Hindoo staying at his home – although doubtless many questioned why he should let such an unkempt Pagan into a Christian dwelling – but knowing about someone is one thing and seeing them in the flesh is quite another entirely. He waved and greeted them all cheerily and they returned the greetings with a look of astonishment, perhaps shocked that such a dark savage could talk. "Yet we are all one," he muttered to himself with a sense of quiet superiority that was, perhaps, not quite in accordance with his religious principles.

He passed the pretty village school where an even prettier schoolmistress was instructing her young charges in algebra and the momentary pang of lust that the sight engendered made him think of his wife Mrinalini in the house where they both lived in Shelidah all those thousands of miles away. One thing that was so striking about the English, even his hostess, the meticulously tidy Mrs. Outram, was how different their marital relationships were. Somehow they seemed more equal; one could never imagine her wiping the dust from her husband's boots. Why was that? Was it perhaps due to the fact that they marry much later in life? Mrina had been but a child when they had wed, so young and innocent. A partnership begun in such a way could never be one of two equals. It was but one of the many things that set India back and yet...

... yet had he not married his own daughters off in the traditional manner at a similar age?

He glanced up again at the schoolmistress, oblivious to his presence as she instructed her young charges and then moved on, descending further down the hill into the very heart of the community. Here a stream actually flooded onto the road and the two were one were a hundred yards or so. Seeing that water reminded Rabin of something and he realised that this was not where he wanted to be. He had been called inwardly to venture out when he could yet, as with so many inward callings, the message had been indistinct. Now though he knew: it had not been the village that had called him, but the river, that most sacred of features. Outram had told him that there was a beautiful valley with both a little river and a little train running down it in the opposite direction to the village and, seeing the water trickle down the main street, now he realised that that was where he was to go. At home it was the mighty Padma, that tributary of the sacred Ganges; here in England he should pay his respects to its tiny cousin. And so it was that he turned about face and retraced his steps back up to the church and the rectory before continuing onwards along the lane that led to the river itself.

The path down was steep, at first only slightly so, then more and more until after half a mile or so, he was scared of slipping over. But the lane was beautiful, fields and hills on either side, like a miniature version of the highlands around Darjeeling which were so precious to him. To his left he could see the river snaking around and alongside it the little railway that Charles had mentioned. There was a train coming down the track, its white smoke puff-puffing out of the funnel of the locomotive. Outram has said that Calthrop, the man who had designed both the railway and the engines had worked in India before and that people thought the little train in the valley looked as though it belonged more in Delhi than Derbyshire. He leaned on a fencepost and watched it pass and saw what they meant; for a few seconds he almost thought he was watching another little train, the one that snakes up to Darjeeling.

By the time that he got to the valley floor, the train had gone and all was silent and still. There was no sign of any life either on the tiny station where it had stopped, nor at the mill over the little stone bridge. He wandered over that bridge and then stood looking at the water running underneath it, a young and lively torrent that caressed the pebbles as it made its way joyfully towards the sea.

Just below the bridge, leading down to the river, were a series of steps. They reminded him of one of the ghats on the Padma in his homeland. Out of instinct, he descended the steps and entered the water, immersing himself in prayer to the Creator who brought into being and is a part of this tiny western river just as much as his mighty eastern one.

He emerged, refreshed, and turned himself around. Behind the mill he spied a small cave in the hillside and, in an instant, he decided to make his way up there to pray and meditate on this beautiful, hidden valley. He climbed up the short distance over land furrowed by generations of sheep but when he arrived at the entrance he was surprised to discover that he was not alone, for sitting there was a man, bearded and with long hair just as he was and wearing coarse robes of natural material. He leaned on a stick and smiled as Rabin approached.

"You're not from round this parts I'll wager," said the man.

Rabin smiled. "No, I come from far away, in India."

The man nodded and smiled back. "I can tell; your prayer practices are not what one would call orthodox. But I like them. God is in that river just as much as He is in any church. Indeed, is not creation His greatest church? That is why I sit here and watch over this valley. It brings me closer to Him."

"You are not here because of your sheep?"

"Me, a shepherd? No, although you could say that I have a flock I suppose. No, I am what you may call a... I don't know really... someone who has withdrawn from the world to be with God."

"In India we would call you a sadhu."

"Then I am a sadhu then! Bertram is the name, and you stranger, what are you called?"

"Rabindranath, Rabindranath Tagore."

"Well, that is a name and a half; I'm not sure if I can remember it, but you're welcome here whatever you may be called. But pray tell me, I am here to worship God; what about you, why have you come to this place?"

Rabin stared out across the green valley below him with its crystal stream and forested slopes. Why was he here? Why had he travelled halfway across the world by steamer to come to this country, the country of the people who oppressed his own? Why had he engaged in debate in Cambridge, met with notables in London and now was staying with a vicar in a small village in the Staffordshire hills?

"I am not sure. To understand perhaps. With everything that I learn, I become aware of more that I do not know. For example, if God is good, then why do men suffer? Why are their millions of people in my homeland who live and die in poverty? Why are women married off as children to men they do not love? Why are there women in their twenties, still young and full of life, who exist as widows, wearing white and shunned by society? Why do white men rule over brown and black men despite the fact that we all bleed red? And why are there so many paths to God and that half of those paths insist that they are the only one?"

They both sat in silence looking out. Rabin noticed that, in the distance, carved into a hillside, was a cave, much larger than the mere cleft in the rock where they now sat.

"I shall tell you my story," said the English sadhu. "It may help you, I don't know. I was like you; a man of wealth and influence, an important figure in the community. But I was unhappy, I sensed that that was not all so I ran away, perhaps like you too are running away from your wife and family now. I ran far away and there I met a girl. She was forbidden to me but love cares not for mere human laws; we were fated to be together if you understand what I mean."

"I think I do. Krishna and Radha never married and yet no love is greater than theirs."

Bertram nodded. "Yes, you do understand," he said quietly. "Anyhow, we ran away together and went to that cave over there, yes, the one you are looking at in the distance. And then, when it was time for her to give birth, I left her to try and find a midwife. And when I returned, she was dead."

"Dead?!"

"A wolf had killed both her and the child. That is when I turned away from this world and embraced my true vocation. I had tried to outrun fate, to escape it. Then I embraced God instead."

"The Christian God?"

"Yes, of course. Although that cave is named after the ancient Norse God of Thunder who was said to have lived there millennia ago so…"

"I understand."

"I know you do."

They sat in silence for some time and then Rabin stood up. "I have to go now; to face fate and fulfil my vocation. Pray for me Bertram!"

"And you me, Rabindranath!"

And with those words he walked back out of the valley and up to the house, his heart as light as air.

---

That evening Mrs. Outram asked her guest if he had made use of the dry weather to explore a little of the area and he told her, "Madam, I felt the river calling to me and so I took a walk down to the valley with the mill where the little train runs."

"Jolly beautiful place," said Charles who had returned from Manchester. "It always reminds me a little of Darjeeling you know!"

"Me also."

"The valley has an interesting history," added Rev. Outram. "There is a cave there named after Thor, the old Viking Thunder God and also legends of our own local saint who lived there over a thousand years ago and converted the locals to the Christian faith."

"Really?" said Rabin. "Pray tell me Reverend, what was his name?"

"Bertram I think. He was some kind of hermit, a bit like your Hindu holy men I suppose; wild hair and beard, healing people and living with the animals, that sort of thing. He was a prince they say who renounced everything after some tragedy befell him. If you like, I can take you to visit his tomb in Ilam, some five or six miles distant."

"Yes Reverend, I should like that very much. To visit the grave of a holy man would be most welcome to me."

And so that following Sunday, after Communion, the entire household took a trip in the carriage across the hills to Ilam. And whilst the others enjoyed a leisurely walk around the grounds of the hall, Rabindranath sat in silent meditation by the tomb of the old Saxon saint. They all thought it was a little strange of course, but then again, he was an Indian, not an Englishman and, well, their ways are so very different.

# Afterword

*Rabindranath Tagore (1861-1941) was arguably the finest Indian man of letters in the 19th and 20th centuries. His words were used for the national anthems of both India and Bangladesh and they also inspired the Sri Lankan national anthem. In 1913 he became the first non-European to win the Nobel Prize for Literature and he was friends with many of the leading literary figures of the day.*

*In 1912 he toured the UK accompanied by Charles F. Andrews, an Anglican clergyman in India who was also close friends with Gandhi. Together they spent some of the summer months staying with the Rev. Outram at the rectory in Butterton, Staffordshire. It is recorded that it rained heavily for much of the trip.*

*Butterton lies only a mile away from the Manifold Valley which has associations with St. Bertram, a 7th century hermit saint who turned to God after a wolf killed his wife and child. He renounced the world and lived in much the same manner as a Hindu sadhu in the area and was buried at Ilam several miles distant from Butterton.*

*Tagore was an intensely spiritual man. He was a Hindu of the Brahmo Samaj school which eschews idols and recognises only one God. In later life he encouraged education in his homeland and founded a university.*

*This story is my attempt to speculate on how his sojourn in my part of the world might have impacted upon this great mind.*

**Written February 2017, Smallthorne, UK**

# Piece of my Heart

The message came when she was sitting in a business meeting. A vibration on her left thigh in the middle of a presentation on the projected development of offshore windfarms. 'Who's messaging me?' she wondered. She pulled out the phone and opened it up.

*So sorry darling, don't know how to tell you this, but I can't continue. I wanted to tell you to your face before you left but I couldn't do it. But I can't delay it any longer. When you come back, I will have moved out. My stuff will be gone. I've found someone else, someone who understands me. We've been struggling for months now, you know that. This way we can both be happy. Love Jens.*

Struggling for months now? How come I am unaware of that? What the hell?! 'But it is all so good, so perfect. Me and Jens works. Me and Jens is good. Jens is so kind, so considerate, so perfect.

Yet perfect men don't dump you by text.

Who dumps their partner by text?

Perfect men don't dump their partners full stop.

When the break came she went to the toilet. She tried to cry but couldn't. Why wouldn't the tears come?

She touched up her make-up anyway.

That evening they had arranged to go out for a meal and a show. Instead she told them that she was feeling ill and to go on without her. She'd stayed in and texted Jens. All the messages had bounced. She'd then phoned his mobile but it was switched off. She was going to call his mum but then froze when she came to punch in the number. What was her number? Why had she never saved it?

She tried to cry again but still the tears wouldn't come.

She put on her coat and walked out.

The crowded streets of London appeared as a dream, snapshots in a haze of unreality – camera-laden tourists, bearded hipsters, a down-and-out asking for money, gays holding hands, Chinese restaurant workers smoking behind their places of work. It was like Scarlett Johannsen walking through Tokyo in 'Lost in Translation'.

What was the name of that character Scarlett played? Pleased to have a problem that she had a hope of solving, she asked her phone. Charlotte, that was it. Charlotte lost in Tokyo, Caroline lost in London.

Tokyo, London. London, Tokyo. A sign saying 'Karaoke'. Perhaps that is the answer? My own little dark space, a private womb of sorrow with...

What to drink...?

...with vodka. Always vodka.

First the vodka. And then...

What to sing?

... then a song by a woman. I am a woman. I am strong. No man will defeat me!

> At first I was afraid
> I was petrified
> I kept thinking I could never live without you
> By my side

That feels good. Gloria knows. Communion between sisters! Sisters are doing it for themselves...

More vodka, more song. No tears but emotion; vomit out that shit from my life, in this numbing haze expunge him from my soul.

> I want you to come on, come on, come on, come on and take it
> Take it!
> Take another little piece of my heart now, baby...

What shit must Janis have been going through when she wrote that?

I know Janis, I understand.

> Oh, oh, break it!
> Break another little bit of my heart now, darling, yeah, yeah, yeah
> Oh, oh, have a!
> Have another little piece of my heart now, baby
> You know you got it if it makes you feel good
> Oh, yes indeed...

*Written 07/03/17, Leek, UK*

# Caféncounters

## *Tokyo, Thursday 27ᵗʰ April, 1995*

It rained on my eightieth birthday. Since I could do little else, I took a ten-minute walk from my apartment to a little café where I had an omelette and salad for lunch. It was on a quiet backstreet near to the Waseda station on the Toden Line and although it was a little more expensive than some of the other places nearby, you could always relax there and the food was good.

I frequented it a lot, particularly when it was raining. It was run by a couple who rarely talked to one another. The gentleman, whose name was Nobu, rarely talked at all whilst the lady, who was called Naoko, rarely shut up. She told me their story once. They were both married, though not to one another. However, they had been married to each other over twenty years before. Seven years later they'd divorced but decided to keep the business going. A seven-year itch that they were still scratching a decade and a half on. I liked that.

As I sat in there, eating by the window, a girl came in. She was about twenty, neatly dressed and took the table by the door. As she ordered her food in painstaking Japanese to Naoko, I looked her up and down. She had long hair and a white cotton mini dress. She also had a pair of sunglasses resting on her forehead, though why considering the weather, I cannot say. She wore a hairslide to the left of her face which she toyed with as she ordered and then, after Naoko had gone away, she dabbed her mouth with her handkerchief. Despite the fact that she had had nothing to eat or drink, I rather liked this little habit of hers which I suspected came from nervousness.

It was only after she had dabbed her mouth for the third time that she looked up and noticed me. I smiled and she smiled back. Could this be one of those brief encounters? "The food here is excellent," I said, in English.

"It is?" Her accent was not that of a native speaker. German, Dutch or Polish perhaps. Some sort of Central European.

"Oh yes, I come here regularly. I live nearby. And you?"

"I am just passing through, travelling. We are in Japan for three weeks."

"We?"

"Yes, I came with a friend, but she has gone to the Tokyo Disneyland today. I wasn't interested so I came here. Haruki Murakami lived around here. He's my favourite author. I want to get a feel for the places that inspired him."

"I am impressed; he is not such a well-known author."

"Not now, but I believe he will be."

There was a silence. She dabbed at her mouth again and then toyed with her hairslide.

"Would you like to join me?" I asked. "I'll buy you a coffee."

"Oh, I don't know, I don't have a huge amount of time and..."

"It's my birthday today. It would be nice to share it a little."

She paused momentarily, weighing up the two options and fiddling with her hairslide and then she smiled and said, "It will be a pleasure, but no coffee."

We talked over coffee and omelette. Her name was Lena and she was from Germany. She had been a student of literature at Stuttgart University but was now having a gap year and seeing a little of the world. It had always been her dream to see Japan. I told her that I was also a student on a gap year and that I also loved travelling. We hit it off straightaway.

Afterwards I took her out. I showed her some of the parks and temples that aren't in the guidebooks. We then went to my favourite public bath which I like for the fact that it is virtually unchanged from the Meiji Era with wooden features in the changing room, a massage chair out of the ark and a fine tiled mural of a mountain scene above the main bath. Or at least, that is the men's section. After we had both exited she told me that the female section was exactly the same and that she loved it; it was the highlight of her trip so far. "This feels like the real Japan, the Japan that Murakami wrote about," she said.

"So you're not regretting Disneyland?" I joked.

Her friend was called Kirsten. She had blonde hair that she plaited into a long pigtail that ran down her back. She was pretty but I preferred Lena with her more unruly brunette mane and captivating, lively face. Kirsten was a little unsure of me at first, which was understandable, but she warmed to me after I took them both to my favourite yakitori joint in Higashi-Shinjuku and then onto a karaoke place where we spent the night drinking and trying to sing. After that there was the decision over where to stay and eventually it was decided that the girls would return to their hotel and I home on the proviso that I met up with them the following morning.

I kept the appointment of course for I had nothing else to do and I had not been so happy in years, but when I got to the hotel, I found that Kirsten had gone out to visit an anime convention that she'd read about in a magazine. Since the weather was still awful, Lena and I stayed in and amused ourselves until Kirsten returned and then I showed them Akihabara and Roppongi, though this time we did not stay out since their flight onwards to Los Angeles departed from Narita the following morning at 11:00. I kissed them both goodbye outside Sushi Nakamura where we'd dined and then left with pleas ringing in my ears for me to visit them both in Germany.

It is rare that I ever do revisit people of course. Those chance encounters are best left as just that. Brief snapshots of reality, stops along the journey of life.

But for Lena I may just make an exception.

## *Stuttgart, Saturday 6th January, 1934*

He was in a café, the only customer. We went in to buy some groceries for the Three Kings Day party that evening and there he was, sitting alone nursing a coffee and writing in his journal. By his side was a German-English dictionary from which I realised that he must be English. What came over me I don't know, but I went over to him, smiled and declared, "How do you do Mr. Brown?"

It was a song you see, a rather silly song, but very popular at the time. "How do you do do Mr. Brown? How do you do do Mr. Brown?" over and over again. As I said, very silly but very catchy too. Anyway, I must have thought that I was being clever. And also that he was very handsome and that I should like to talk with such a handsome chap but that I had nothing else to say and so Mr. Brown stepped in.

Oh, we were young then, I, my friend Annie and he also. His name was Michael and his face lit up when I spoke to him. He liked us as much as we liked him. He spoke in English but then realised that the inane Mr. Brown line was as far as ours stretched, so then he switched to German which he spoke rather well. "Please, stay!" he said, standing up and offering us chairs. "Let me buy you both a coffee."

Annie, who was rather embarrassed by my calling out to this stranger (but at the same time, just as curious about him as I) replied, "No, no, many thanks, but we must go." But then he looked so sad that we relented and agreed to stay, but not the coffee.

He told us that he was nineteen and was walking across Europe. That sounded awfully exciting as you can imagine. I told him that we were also nineteen and students, I from Donaueschingen and Lise from here. He asked why we were buying so many cakes and groceries and so we explained about the party and then, in another fit of impetuosity, I invited him along. And so he drained his coffee and came with us.

I was staying at Annie's place then, of course, and, thankfully, her parents were away (what on earth they would have said about us inviting stray handsome young men back I dare not think). We took him there, telling him that he could sleep on the sofa before then smartening him up for the party.

The party itself was a grand affair, lots of food and singing songs. We introduced him as Mr. Brown of course, a friend of my family, and he treated us to a rather queer English hymn about the Three Kings. But it was after the main event and back in the apartment that the real fun was to be had. We all changed into our pyjamas – he wore a set belonging to Annie's father – and we sat and talked and drank wine until the early hours. He was such excellent company and both Annie and I were taken with him and I do confess that, when she left to answer the call of nature, we did steal a kiss that was so heavenly... and... there was nothing more than that, all innocent fun.

The next day it rained, buckets coming down, a typical miserable January day. We'd planned to go walking but obviously that wasn't possible and we arose too late for church also. Annie teased me about that, saying that I should be going to confession – that was a reference to the kissing as I am sure she realised – but that Michael replied that we had nothing to confess since we had sheltered the needy, fed the hungry and clothed the naked. Ha! Ha! Anyway, we stayed in, playing records on the gramophone, 'St. Louis Blues', 'Stormy Weather', that kind of thing.

Around eleven Annie and Michael left, she to luncheon with relatives and he to buy some clothes since we were all invited to a rather grand party at the home of von Schnitzler, a wealthy industrialist Annie's family knew. Michael returned pretty soon though – I think he'd just bought the first outfit he saw although I must admit that it suited him – and we did what we had so wished to do the previous night.

By the time Annie returned he was sketching me and it all looked very innocent. He did a sketch of her afterwards that was a remarkable likeness.

The party that night was hilarious. We were picked up in a great Mercedes and whisked away to von Schnitzler's home, a large concrete place of hideous taste. Our host, who was both an outright Nazi and an admirer of both Annie and I, took an instant dislike to Michael whom he referred to disparagingly as "The English Globetrotter" but our Mr. Brown played his part well and protected us from the oaf. At one point he had us cornered and was paying us sycophantic compliments like, "You two remind me of the two graces" at which point Michael jumped in and declared, "And now there are three!"

We returned to the apartment afterwards for more dancing, drinking and jollity although that was all there was to it and the next morning we bade him goodbye, our darling Mr. Brown, and I never saw him again after that although, I must admit, many times over the years, I have wondered what became of him.


# Café, Saturday 27<sup>th</sup> April, 1944

It was in a café. But where else could it be? Why a café? Because they are places between worlds. Not here and not there. People wait in them on railway stations, services by the highway, sad seafronts and happy high streets, nursing mugs of tea or coffee. They are neither one place nor another, no one's home, no one's destination, merely a place to pause on the endless journey.

A non-place.

So too was this café. Plain wooden tables crowned with salt, pepper and vinegar; generic prints on the walls, an urn bubbling in the background. I ordered a tea from the counter and waited, the oozing of the blood, the heat of the battle and the memory of the pain still fresh in my head.

When he arrived, he smiled, ordered a drink for himself and then came to join me. "Peter," he said, holding out his hand as if he needed any introduction. I shook it of course. He didn't look like he did in the hundreds of paintings and statues that I'd seen of him but then he was never depicted meeting people in a café either. "Sorry that you've had to wait," he said, "I'm a bit overrun at the moment. Anyway, how are you?"

I told him that I was fine, all things considering.

"Indeed, I know what you mean," he replied. "These are funny times that we're in at the moment," he added.

"Look Peter," I said, "what's going to happen from here? We tried our best with that mission you know; it was just awful bad luck that Sandy got spotted and the Germans ambushed us and..."

"I'm not bothered about the mission. That is in the past. My job is to look forward."

"So what now then?"

"That depends on you." He put his tea down and eyed me intently. He had large, dark eyes, deep and penetrating. They reminded me a little of the eyes of some of the Cretans that I'd fought with.

"Tell me, Michael, what do you want?"

"Well, do I qualify to get in?"

"Qualification is my department, so don't worry about it. Let me put it another way, if I could offer you anything what would you go for?"

I stirred another sugar into my now luke-warm tea and thought. "Well, do you know what; I've never been happier than when just wandering around, going from place to place, stopping off in random towns and having chance encounters with people."

"Give me an example."

"Before the war I was in Stuttgart, in a café, and two German girls came in. We got talking and I went back to their place with them. We went to a kids' party that night, then some meal the next. We danced to gramophone records and we grew very close. It was perhaps the happiest time of my life. For a few hours our lives converged, two trains running on parallel tracks and then off they diverged again, to different destinations, never to meet again. It was beautiful. Was it the Buddha who said we should have no attachments and live in the moment?"

"He and others. Very well then, if that is what you want, then go ahead, stay here and do that."

"I can?"

"Who is the boss here, you or me?"

"For how long?"

"I'll let you know when."

"You sure?"

"You'll know when anyway."

"Thanks Peter."

"Don't mention it, Michael."


## *Donaueschingen, Saturday 16th December, 1995*

"Lena, who is this?"

"Oh, that is the boy that I met in Japan. The one that I was telling you about. He was in a café and we got talking."

"The one that you rather liked?"

"Yes, that is the one. I received it in a letter off him that arrived yesterday. Here it is. He says that he's going to come to see me in Stuttgart."

"Does he now? What was his name again?"

"Michael, gran."

## Stuttgart, Saturday 6th January, 1996

He was in the café, the only customer. There he was, sitting alone nursing a coffee and writing in his journal. I went over to him, smiled and declared, "How do you do Mr. Brown?"

He smiled, stood up and looked me in the eyes. "Please, stay!" he said, standing up and offering me a chair. "Let me buy you a coffee."

I accepted the invitation. "Well, just for five minutes," I said.

The coffee came and I stirred a sugar into it. "You have changed," he said.

"You haven't," I replied.

"Externally, perhaps so," he said and then, looking up, asked, "How is Annie?"

A momentary shadow clouded my mind as I pictured her grave, that sad funeral twenty years before. He must have seen it for he did not pursue the matter further.

"I believe that you met my granddaughter in Tokyo," I said.

"Lena is your granddaughter? Makes sense. And it explains how you got my address. I don't know normally give it out."

"Why did you this time?"

"I can't say exactly. Something told me that I should."

The door opened and a man entered. He looked tired and overworked. Michael gestured to him and he came over.

"I wondered when you'd be joining us," he said.

"Yes, here I am. Sorry I'm a little late. The usual."

"Last time we came here it was me who had a friend," I said.

"Please, let me introduce Peter."

"Nice to meet you, Lise," said the newcomer.

"How do you know my name?" I asked, knowing the answer already.

And because he knew that I knew the answer, he didn't bother to answer.

"Let me buy you a coffee," said Michael.

"No, no, many thanks, but we must go," he replied.

I nodded and so did Michael. We drained our cups and then he got up, coming round to my side to help me up like the gentleman that he was.

"Don't worry," said Peter, seeing how unsteady on my feet I was. "It's not far."

*Written 8th March, 2017, Leek, UK*

# The Sun of the Nation

# 男

They call me the Sun of the Nation. I am not. I am only the moon, but a pale reflection of Her glories.

Fill my glass again. I need another drink.

I can still see clearly, as clearly as if it were yesterday, that moment when we met. We were out of the Motherland at the time, at the Sandaowan base in Yanji Province. It was a sorry place, bleak and Spartan. There was no joy there, no colour. And it was cold. Boy, was it cold! But then She walked into the room. Comrade Jong-Suk, the young woman in charge of the Children's Corps. Of course, I had heard about Her, but nothing had registered. She was no more than a glorified nursemaid after all. But when She stepped into that room my heart stopped and so too, I believe, did Hers.

She was eighteen. So young, fresh and innocent. I was only twenty-three myself of course. Yet life had made me hard and bitter. I later learned that She too had known intolerable hardships, yet it never showed on Her face. And in all the years that we were together, the one thing that continually pressed itself upon me was Her innocence. She had purity and optimism. The first thing that I thought of when I saw Her was of Mary whom I heard so much about from my father and the Christian teachers at school. Hail Jong-Suk full of grace, the Lord is with Thee. Blessed art Thou amongst women...

...and blessed is the fruit of Thy womb...

Yes, I know that sounds strange in today's Korea, the land where we have eliminated such superstitious and backward thinking. And that has been more down to me than anyone else! Yet it is true, I did think of Mary. You won't know the story but the Bible talks about an angel appearing to her. Sadly for Jong-Suk she met no angel, only me. And yet, I do believe that She somehow confused the two.

Fill my glass up!

---

We present things as being good or bad, right or wrong, black or white. Comrade Pak Pong-Ju gave his self-criticism today. He knelt and grovelled before the room, before me, tears pouring from his eyes. He had to; he had no choice. Not that it will help him. My heart is not completely cold though. His wife and children will be spared. Choi-An reminds me a little of Her actually, only slightly but it is there. Choi-An passes you at a party and for a split second you are mistaken. Could it be...? It is not, of course. She is but a pale imitation. Even so, it is nice. And if she has but an eighth of Jong-Suk's purity, then she should be spared.

No, Pak Pong-Ju must die. I know that, he knows that. It is for the greater good. He has admitted to evil and so must be punished for it. But really, is anyone truly bad or good? Is there black or white? Comrade Pak Pong-Ju is a good case in point. In the beginning he was motivated by the suffering of the peasants. I recall him first joining our band, wide-eyed and full of hatred towards the oppressors. Yet now that we have driven them from our shores and subdued the landlords and other class enemies, built a strong and stable nation in which the people can flourish, now he has changed. He likes luxury too much and he thinks not of the people in general but instead only those whom he is related to. He is more concerned with securing a position for his son rather than liberation for the masses. He is not good and not bad. He is human.

I too am human. I know that all too well.

But Her? No, She was different. She was like Mary. Spotless. Pure. A shining sun of goodness. The sun of right over wrong that drove our revolution forwards.

And on nights like this, after so many glasses of soju that I struggle to count them I wonder: did perhaps that revolution die with Her?

---

Death. What a sad death She endured. Pain and anguish as She gave birth to a daughter whose eyes would never open. There is no shame in such a death, nor novelty. Women have died in that way ever since the beginning of time. But there is sadness. That a life that was never meant to be should snuff out a fire that burned so brightly. The scene afterwards was like a murder. Blood everywhere. It was a murder. That is why I gave orders for it to be kept quiet. It was a private, not public affair. I gave Her that dignity.

---

And as I sit here and let you pour me another soju I know that, like that bottle in your hand, my life is also running dry. I do not mind. I have lived for many years and fulfilled my destiny. As a young man I dreamed of changing the world and I have done that. Now I dream only of the day when I close my eyes and am reunited with Her. Not in heaven of course, we communists cannot expect that, although I must admit, I do hope. No, at least lain side-by-side in death as we did in life. Yet even that will be denied to me. Dogma and protocol decree that I must lie alone in state, for the good of the nation, as an example to inspire them, as a focus for their devotions. But She will not be there. She lies alone in the Martyrs' Cemetery on Mt. Taesong, forever waiting for her angel to come.

And She was a martyr. There is no doubt about that.

With power comes pain.

And loneliness.

When She died on that chilly September day, a part of me died also. And that which remained was changed. I have often thought about it. We navigate differently by the sun than the moon. When the sun is high in the sky, it is easy. When only the moon is there, we need a lamp.

And if the sun can be extinguished once, then we know it can happen again. In my grief I realised that I could rely on no one and nothing, only myself. Self-reliance. Juche. Looking back I realise that September 22nd, 1949 was the day it was born. I never mentioned it to the world until a full five years later but that was the day when the seed was germinated. How ironic; She died giving birth to the future of the nation but the child that She bore was not the one in her womb. Instead it was the new lamp to lead us on our way.

But can a lamp ever equal the light of the sun?

And is that bottle completely done? Fetch another!

Yes, and you shall have one too. Go on... all the way to the top...

She was marvellous you know, in those days. I don't want to think about Her death, how She was in that room, just as I do not want to think about my life now, here, aged and broken, half-addled on this damned liquor, waiting to die, waiting for my son... our son... to take over... and fuck it all up most likely. He doesn't get things like I do and these are difficult times. He is Her son; reality doesn't come into it with him. She believed that anything was possible so long as you wanted it enough. He is the same. The only difference is that She was pure and Her desires reflected that untainted soul. His, on the other hand, are stained and selfish. He is Her son but he is mine as well. Ha!

But no, when I think of Her I think of those days fighting in the forest; the days when we had nothing except hope and comradeship. We had nothing to lose too. I recall with joy that day when She came to our camp bearing that steaming pot of stew that She had carried for miles on her head, the boiling iron pot burning Her and weighing Her down. Yet She never complained and She carried out her duty like a true soldier.

And when she sewed all those uniforms for the partisans, working late into the night when she could hardly see a thing, stitching and sewing carefully. And they were all perfect and fitted like gloves. I bet you couldn't do that, eh, could you? Can you sew like she could? Of course not; next to her you are a fucking waste of space, a useless whore…

… as am I…

…as are we all.

Like I said, she was the Sun.

Fuck it! Drink up and refill and then move closer next to me. When I put my arm around you I am reminded of those halcyon nights sat around the campfire in the bleak hellhole that was Vyatskoye. She would lean her head on my shoulder and tell me about the hard life that she endured in Hoeryong, how the landlords beat her parents, and of the bright new world that we would create together.

The dream that I have now turned into a reality…

…perhaps.

Oh yes, you are just one of many. I'm sorry if that makes you pout my pretty little rabbit, but it's true! Both before her and after her, even another wife. Some even more beautiful, in the eyes of the world at least. But beauty is more than just looks; the heart has a greater beauty than the eyes or the hips. And her heart was unmatched. Do you know what, after the liberation, she was not interested in retribution at all. Other comrades clamoured to kill this traitor or humiliate that one, but all those things, they did not interest her in the slightest. Instead all she thought about was what we could now build: hospitals, universities, kindergartens... places of healing and learning. She built, others destroyed. I destroyed. I am human after all. As are you, as are all of you. Pale copies of the genuine article. Cheap prints of an ink painting by Owon.

You turn from me and I know why. I am drunk and I am old and ugly. No, not my skin or my wretched body; that is not what I talk of nor what you turn from. My mind. I was good once, pure once. Not like her but my heart was full of noble dreams. I was the man my propagandists claim I was... and still am. But age gets in the way, power too, jealousy, hatred, envy. All the sins. My father used to talk of sin and the devil. As a child he warned me that the devil can tempt anyone, make even the best man do evil. Like that great king David who saw Bathsheba bathing and wanted her for himself. I've often thought about that story. You don't even know what I'm talking about, do you? You're asleep anyway. Better that way. As a youth I wondered what that Bathsheba looked like; what a temptress had to look like to steer such a holy man as David away from his God. Later in life I learned of course. No, not you. You are more like one of Solomon's hundreds of concubines. I can't even remember your name and even by tomorrow your breasts, hips, eyes and other alluring features will have merged with the hundreds of others that I've taken.

No, I'm talking about her. Not Her, but her. The one who came to the camp afterwards. The one who had the external beauty. The one who spoke sweet and honeyed words. My Bathsheba. The one who drew me away from my God.

The one whom I was lying with on that fateful night when she bled to death alone giving birth to our lifeless child. The yin to her yang, the night to her day. The one who convinced me not to call for a doctor when she could have been saved.

The one whom I married afterwards.

The one who taught me the other truth of self-reliance.

Fuck it! This bottle is empty too, and you are asleep. I could wake you but in truth I have had too much already. When you're sleeping so peacefully, I can believe in your purity too. It is an illusion but a beautiful one nonetheless.

No, I shall not stay here watching your breasts rise and fall. It is disrespectful to her memory. Instead I shall walk to the window and watch the sun rise over the bed of pink azaleas that I had planted there. Azaleas were her favourite flower. She said they reminded her of the spring. Of the fact that all that is cold, desolate and dead, will be born anew. That tomorrow will be brighter than today.

Yet I shall not live to see that new day.

And that, perhaps, is no bad thing.

*Written August 7th, 2017, Birmingham New Street – Stoke-on-Trent, UK*

# The Sun of the Nation

女

Then I was young. Then I was in the early dawn of adulthood, waiting for the sun of maturity to rise. At that age you can believe in perfection. Until very recently, I still did.

You wouldn't be able to comprehend the impression that he made on me then. He was strong, handsome, confident and brimming full of his beliefs. When I first set eyes upon him in that camp at Sandaowan he had a smile on his lips and a twinkle in his eyes. I'd heard about him and his magnetism beforehand, off female comrades who spoke, wide-eyed, of him in hushed tones. I was excited and nervous as I approached the camp. The moment I set eyes upon him I was besotted. He exceeded all my high expectations. He was the Sun of the Nation. I was young and in love.

Arrgh! These pains are becoming more frequent... and unbearable. It will not be long now. I am scared.

What did he see in me? I've wondered about that ever since. Some people call me beautiful but I know I'm not. I am dumpy; that is what my mother said and those words have always made me conscious of the fact. My legs are too short and fat and my shoulders too broad. I am a plain peasant girl, nothing more. He could have had other girls; before me he had plenty of other girls. So what did he see in me? I believe it was the vision. He shared my vision. I shared his vision. We fell in love, not with each other, but the vision.

Breathe deeply, breathe deeply. It is coming. Think of something happier; take you mind away from things...

There was no time happier than those years that we spent together with nothing. Sitting around the campfire, far from our homeland in chilly Vyatskoye, holding hands and talking about our vision, the future that we would build. Together. I remember leaning my head against his shoulder and holding a pressed azalea in my hand. And he asked me why I carried that flower and I replied that it reminded me of my beautiful hometown of Hoeryong to which we would one day return, and of the fact that this winter is not eternal and that spring will come. The deaths of all those fine young comrades will not be in vain.

"Yes," he replied, "we shall get our revenge."

And that, looking back, was perhaps the first sign. Revenge, my love, why do you think of revenge? Think instead of what we shall build, not destroy.

Arrgh! It was come again. Breathe! Breathe! It will pass. All things pass. Azaleas signal that winter passes to spring...

Our marriage was simple. It was beautiful. A marriage of the vision, the dream, the future. We stood side-by-side, both wearing our partisan's uniforms and were clapped by our comrades. Afterwards they drank a lot of soju. He drank a lot of soju. I forgave it of course. As the years passed I forgave things more and more.

Back then he was like a god to me, my idol. What I did for him, I did for the revolution, the vision. I sewed uniforms through the night for the men; I carried a boiling stew pot to the frontline on my head and suffered burns and headaches afterwards; I even fired a gun in anger and killed people. In combat though, only in combat. All for him, all for the vision.

If asked to, I would have given my life.

Arrrrgh, oh God, here it comes again! Longer and more acute this time. How shall I bear it? How long shall this tidal wave of agony last? Why me?

The thoughts of revenge did not go away. Nor too did the jealousy and the hatred. I calmed them... and him. And after I did he would squeeze me hand and thank me, telling me that I was the sun in his sky. I laughed and replied, "No, it is you that is the sun for this nation. But you don't have to rely on yourself all the time. Trust people a little more, my love, do not hate them."

Yet the very next day we fought a battle and captured some landlords. I could not watch what he did to them.

And with each massacre, he receded from me.

Relief. It recedes... for now.

I thought that the baby would change things between us. He did. He was so beautiful. I have never felt such love and happiness as when I clasped his tiny body in my arms and shielded him from the northern cold. Oh yes, he changed things, but not as I had imagined. I had a new sun in my sky now and the old one drifted away. He spent time with her.

Her. The moment she arrived I knew she was trouble! A woman can tell. She was his type. Pretty eyes espousing high ideals. Not dumpy. I knew he was tempted. I clung to him all the more. He drank all the more.

Then there was a change. After the breastfeeding finished and when the fighting began to draw to a close. We both decide to mend things. We came together, held hands, went for walks, made love. But he had changed. The hatred had grown along with that obsession with revenge. She had fed his hunger. Abstract anger had become concrete cruelty. The intimacy between us which had before been natural was now forced.

Arrrgh! Here it comes again! How many more times? Be strong, girl! Be strong!

The days of triumph were the days of defeat. I was happy, I believed it. As we travelled towards Pyongyang on that old freight train and greeted the peasants at every stop, I shared their joy, hugged them, reassured them, danced with them. He though, stood back, aloof, observing from afar. And she was always in the shadows. He had lost his connection with the people, with the vision. I told myself that all would come good. In my heart though, I knew I was lying.

Arrrgh! Oh God, please spare me! Make this the last please! It is intolerable! Give me strength! The pain! The pain! The pain…

I am calmer now. It was receded once more. That was not the final time.

It wasn't all bad you know. There was great work done and he gave me free rein to do it. Schools, hospitals, universities and clinics. The vision was being built! Abstract became reality. I worked with my hands, knee-deep in the mud on the project to prevent flooding on the Pothong, the River of Disaster as the peasants called it.

He was not there. He allowed it but he was not interested in it.

Instead he became cold and dedicated his time to military matters even though we had won.

And to building camps.

Arrgh! It comes again, as sure as day follows night. And this one is the final one. I feel it in my bones.

My time has come. I know it. This baby inside of me is already dead. A mother can sense these things. And it will kill me in the process. I am only twenty-nine and that is no age to die. I am still young with so much to do.

And yet... I am not sad. I do not fear it; I welcome it. I am glad. Does that sound deranged? Perhaps I am. Perhaps the decomposing body inside my womb is poisoning my mind. But I am glad. If he sends for his doctor – if he remembers too while cavorting with her in our bed – I shall refuse him. I have already locked and barricaded the door. This is my destiny.

For it is not the baby inside of me that has died, but the vision. We gave birth to it when it was already dead and I cannot bear to see it putrefy and decay further. It hurts too much.

I am at heart a simple peasant, the child of simple peasants, and so I live as a simple peasant does.

My sun has set and so I must turn in for the night and sleep.

And when I close my eyes I shall dream of azaleas on the hills around Hoeryong.

***Written 9th August, 2017, Birmingham, UK***

# Laying the Foundations of the New Albania

I first saw her on the xhiro, that parade of souls that we Illyrians have partaken in every evening since Illyrius set up his kingdom in these mountains. I was not long back from Sweden and was walking with my old friend Vaso. I saw her but I think she saw me first. Our eyes locked for a moment and a thousand words were left unspoken. Then she passed on by and I did not see her for the rest of the xhiro.

But the following evening she was there again, then the next and then the next. I asked Vaso her name but he did not know it. Another friend said that she played volleyball for the national team so I went to watch their next game. Her name was Silva Turdiu. The name meant nothing to me then; only her smile and laughing eyes mattered. After the game I approached her. She recognised me immediately. On the xhiro that evening I shared a coffee with her, not Vaso. Our balcony and walled garden was Dëshmorët e Kombit Boulevard, Tiranë.

Three weeks later I approached my father. "I've found a girl I want to marry," I told him. The joy, nay, relief, on his face was palpable. A smile full of the glories of socialism spread across it. "What is her name?" he asked.

"Silva."

"And her family?"

"Turdiu."

The smile vanished. Imperialist infiltration. Titoist mischief.

I knew why. When I'd mentioned Silva to my brother Bashkim, he'd asked the same question. And when I'd pronounced the syllables Tur-diu he had taken a sharp intake of breath and replied, "It might as well be Capulet!"

Father was more positive. "We can overcome this," he said the following day. "Her record is spotless."

"But her father!" protested mum.

"Prof. Qasim Turdiu has an unreliable record it is true, but he has never been purged."

"And her mother's relative?"

"Arshi Pipa is an enemy of the people, that is without doubt, but his connection to her is distant and he is far away in America. I give my consent."

"Had you not better check with Comrade Enver first?" she warned, pleaded.

"Comrade Enver is on holiday in Pogdarec enjoying a well-earned break. He would not wish to be disturbed over such a trivial matter."

"But..."

"But nothing! Am I or am I not head of this family and prime minister of this country? I give my consent! Congratulations Shkënder my son!"

And he was right. He was the head of the family and the prime minister of the country and the first people to congratulate us were Comrade Enver and Comrade Nexhmije. They came round to our house as soon as they returned from Pogdarec and sat either side of Silva as if they were her minders. She was all smiles, feted so by the man who was Albania and his elegant wife. I was as proud as a partisan.

A couple of days later Comrade Enver called my father into a meeting.

His face when he returned said it all.

His self-criticisms and the grovelling apologies that he made afterwards sullied his glory.

The cold shoulders that we received from all our "friends" stung like a hornet's nest.

But that pain was nothing to what I felt when I had to tell my darling that our engagement was off.

"I have known Comrade Enver for over forty years yet I have never felt that I could call him a friend; I don't believe anyone can," father said to me.

That night he shot himself.

---

I first saw her on the xhiro, that parade of souls that we Ilyrians have partaken in every evening since Illyrius set up his kingdom in these mountains. I was not long back from Sweden and was walking with my old friend Vaso. I saw her but I think she saw me first. Our eyes locked for a moment and a thousand words were left unspoken. Then she passed on by and I did not see her for the rest of the xhiro.

I knew it was her right away. It was true that old Carpenter Time had been to work on her features, sanding them into something rougher. But still that glorious soul shone through. That night I lay awake thinking of her, of me, of what should have been.

The following evening she was there again. I stopped her and she smiled. For the first time in twenty years we shared a coffee.

"How are you?"

"I am well. And you?"

"Also."

A pause. A long, pregnant pause, although not as long as the last one. That pause of decade filled with labour and grieving.

"Are you married?"

"Yes, since 1987. We have two children. And you?"

"Yes, I'm married also, although not for so long."

We paused again and looked into one another's eyes. Carpenter Time had not reworked those. This time she spoke first: "They let you live."

"Yes, although I'm unsure why. Father died... and my brother."

"I know, it was in the newspapers."

"I forgot." Another pause. "We – mother and I – were sent off to prison, Burrel. Twenty-five years, enemies of the people. It killed my mum. We were released when the regime fell."

"I'm sorry."

I shrugged. "We were far from the only ones."

She nodded. "We were exiled, to a prefab in Lapraka. I was dismissed from both university and the national team. I spent years making socks, shunned by everyone."

"I'm sorry."

She shrugged.

"I went abroad after the change, to Sweden. I could get a visa since I'd studied there before. I couldn't bear being in this place so I started a new life."

"And I married and together we emigrated to America. Same story. We needed a fresh start."

"So we're both just back for a holiday then."

She smiled. What more was there to say? "It was lovely to see you Shkënder," she whispered.

"You too Silva. May you have a long life!" I meant it.

"You too. I believe that she meant it as well.

---

I sat there for the rest of that evening sipping my coffee and watching the people pass by. Young people glancing at one another with desire as we had once done; old people holding hands after a lifetime of togetherness. A lifetime denied to us. An anger welled up inside me, a hatred for Comrade Enver and his paranoia. What gave him the right to destroy my life like that? How dare he!

Yet, I reflected as I slowly stirred the dregs in my drained cup, what I had suffered was nothing. I had lived the good life because my father had been as ruthless and empty as Comrade Enver. And my punishment had been nothing compared to all those thousands who served their full terms of twenty-five years or more or who, like my mother, father and brother, eventually paid the ultimate price for their sins. The hollow wrecks, nameless and friendless who I had seen fall by the wayside at Burrel or shot against a crude brick wall.

And as I sat there stirring, the number of people walking the xhiro before me multiplied, ten-fold, a hundred-fold, and joining the ranks of the living were all those, including my own soul, who had perished laying the foundations of the new Albania.

*Written 30th-31st August, 2017, Deniz Houses Hotel, Istanbul, Turkey*

# Confirmed by History

Captain Kang Hong-Sik leaned back in the chair outside his office and took a long drag of his cigarette. This was his favourite time of the day, that magical hour when the working day began to draw to a close. His eyes skirted over the scene before him: red-neckerchief-clad children returning from school; old Mun Ye-Bong guiding his equally ancient bullock and cart along the road; the grain growing lush and green in the fields, the heads blowing in the breeze while every so often a bent back betrayed the presence of a farmworker; the co-operative's little red tractor chugging along the lane; the pine-forested slopes beyond; the clear blue sky above and, in the distance, the large mosaic picture of the President depicting him inspecting a bountiful harvest. All was as it should be, all was good, all was well in the little town of Chongpyong.

He took another drag and bent down to pick up his beaker of tea. Then his eyes caught something, something amiss. It was a bicycle, a bicycle carrying the unmistakable figure of Police Officer Choe Ik-Kyu of the nearby village of Jaean-ri. And it was heading straight for the station. With a sigh, Hong-Sik stood up, stubbed out his cigarette in the ash tray and came down to meet his subordinate. "Comrade Ik-Kyu, what brings you here?" he asked in a tone that was trying hard to be jovial.

"Com...rade... Cap... tain," wheezed the out-of-breath policeman. "Mur... der! There's been a... murder! In Jaean-ri! Come quick!"

---

The sight before him made his stomach turn. In voluntarily Hong-Sik turned away and vomited all over the packed earth. As he did so he noticed the dried remnants of an earlier vomiting, most likely Ik-Kyu's.

The body... no, it was hardly that. Or at least, he could see very little body. This was due to it being buried up to the neck in the ground, doubtless when its owner was still alive. And of that which protruded, namely the head, there was little left. Cause of death: it had been kicked repeatedly until it was attached to the body by old a slither of skin and sinew. It was a ruddy pulp and was now covered in flies.

"Who was he?"

Officer Ik-Kyu pointed at the adjacent house. "He lived there. Name was Pak Kil-Yon. He'd only just moved here... from Pyongyang. No one knew him."

"Political?"

"Don't think so. We haven't had the file yet but from what the escort said, more pisshead that political."

Hong-Sik sighed. Typical. Some pissed-up oaf who can't do his job because he's got an alcohol problem and Pyongyang decide to exile him here. We're always the dumping ground for the useless. "Who knows about this?"

"Only the postman. He found him when delivering a letter."

"Make sure no one else knows. Seal the place off!"

"Yes Comrade Captain!"

"And who knows him best round here?"

"Only his work group leader, Comrade No Kum-Sok."

"Where's he live?"

---

"That prick? Fuck me, Comrade Captain, what d'you wanna know about him for? Waste of space the man was. Always pissed. Reckon that's why they dumped him on us. Bloody typical. Pyongyang has a problem and Chongpyong has to sort it out."

"So he was a native of Pyongyang then?"

"Nah, I dinna say that, Comrade Captain. Pyongyang sent him here, but he wasn't no Pyongyanger."

"How do you know?"

"His accent. He had a weird fucking accent. Not local, not Pyongyang, but something like I've never heard before. That said though – and here's the weird bit – sometimes it did sound a bit local, like he'd know phrases in our dialect and that, but mostly it was just weird. Never heard an accent like that one before!"

"And may you never again Comrade Kum-Sok, although if I were you I'd ponder more your attitude towards our great capital city and the people who populate it and make decisions for us. After all, the General Himself comes from Pyongyang."

A momentary cloud of fear crossed the face of the work group leader. Hong-Sik would never have done anything but it was useful to have such a manner of control at his fingertips.

"Yes, err, Comrade Captain, I will consider that... I will indeed."

---

Hong-Sik knew that he would have to go to Hamhung and the sooner the better. Before anything else he needed to see that file and if it was anywhere, it was there. So, he jumped on the station's motorbike and rode straight off. At the county checkpoint though, there was an eager new conscript on the gate.

"Pass!" he rapped.

"What?"

"Pass, Comrade. No one may pass through here without authorisation. Where is your pass?"

"I don't have one, now let me through!"

"No pass, no entry. And you are to address me as Comrade!"

"Am I really? Oh, I do apologise Comrade Private, but pray tell me, where might one get this pass from?"

"From the police of course. Is this some kind of a joke...?"

"Well, I am the fucking police, here's my badge and so fuck off and let me through!"

"Comrade Captain, I apologise, I didn't realise..."

But by that time Hong-Sik had already disappeared in a cloud of dust.

---

"Murdered by having his head kicked off! That's barbaric! Glad I didn't have to witness that!" For the first time in his professional career, Hong-Sik thought his superior, Inspector Li Byong-Uk looked genuinely concerned for him.

"Glad for you that you didn't Comrade Inspector, but you're right, it was barbaric, pure barbarism, but who would kill in such a way. If you wanted to murder someone, just slog them round the head with a metal bar or hang them or something, but burying them up to the neck in the ground and kicking their head off, now that is something else."

"The work of a single man?"

"I'm no pathologist, but I'd say several. The kicks were landed from all angles."

"Queer and gruesome affair all round. We need to keep this hush-hush, reflects badly on us otherwise. Any ideas who might be the killer?"

"None, but the file makes for interesting reading. Pak Kil-Yon, aged fifty-eight, exiled here from Pyongyang two weeks ago due to persistent alcoholism, failing to attend work parties and so on. However, he was no

Pyongyanger; two years ago he emigrated to the DPRK from Japan where he was a long-standing member of Chongryon. Had always been an exemplary supporter of our country while in Japan, regularly sending remittances and never having a single ideological bad mark against his name. Here though, it was just drinking, drinking and more drinking, plus attempts to corrupt his neighbours and work colleagues through gambling for money. And, get this, it states that when he found out that his destination was to be near Chongpyong he pleaded to be sent somewhere else although he gave no reason as to why."

"Probably because to a man from Pyongyang and Tokyo, this is about as back of beyond as you can get."

"Probably."

"So, you've no suspects, no motive and no clue."

"In short, yes."

"Well, get me all three. I've no doubt that you can. Fancy a drink first though?"

"Yes, although... I thought that while I'm here, I'd like to pay my respects to the General. After that though."

"You're a good citizen Comrade Kang Hong-Sik."

'But do good citizens have what it takes to solve murders by very bad citizens?' he thought to himself.

---

Hong-Sik stood before the great bronze statue and gazed up at it. Then he took three steps forward and bowed deeply for several seconds before straightening himself again and taking three steps back. He gazed into the eyes, those famous, loving, wise eyes that had guided his homeland from utter destruction and ruin to a land of socialist plenty. 'What would you do?' he asked the General silently. The general smiled back, omnipotent, omniscient and omnipresent. Hong-Sik walked over to the nearby pagoda and sat silently watching the bustling city below. His grandfather, the greatest influence on his life, had been a devout Buddhist in his youth. Later, during the Anti-Japanese Struggle he had changed. The suffering changed him. "Where was the Buddha in all that hatred and misery, that is what I asked myself," he had told his grandson. "I could believe in the supernatural no more, but the communists, the partisans, the General, now they were real and did do something. You could say that I transferred my allegiance and I do not regret doing so. But one thing of the Buddhism stayed with me: the importance of meditation. Always take time to sit in silence, alone and collect your thoughts. Suddenly the clouds disperse and you can clearly see the path ahead."

Hong-Sik had taken his grandfather at his word and had always tried to follow that advice. He did so now for he needed the clouds to disperse. Instead though, his mind kept getting pulled back to the statue of the General, as if Comrade Kim Il-Sung Himself were trying to tell him something. Kim Il-Sung and his grandfather. The Anti-Japanese Struggle, the cruelty, misery and suffering. Into his head came a saying of the General's:

'The oppressed peoples can liberate themselves only through struggle. This is a simple and clear truth confirmed by history.'

In an instant the clouds dispersed and he saw clearly the path ahead.

---

The following day, back in Chongpyong, he went to visit Pak Yong-Ho. Yong-Ho was his grandfather's former friend and one of the oldest men in the village. "Tell me about the time of the Japanese occupation," he said.

Old Yong-Ho looked into the middle distance and spat absent-mindedly on the floor. "They were hard times, unbelievably cruel and barbaric. We were nothing to them, like animals. They killed Koreans for fun. With my own eyes I saw six innocent men lined up against that very wall over there and shot. And their crime? Stealing rice to feed their families. They called it treason against the state. Animals!"

"Did they always shoot their victims?"

"No, not at all. They bayoneted some, beat others to death. In the village of Jaean-ri over yonder they took all the men of one family, buried them up to their necks in the ground and then kicked their heads off which they then used to play football. And what is worse, they made the women and children watch."

"What family was that?"

"The Yu family. The son – he was about four at the time – still lives there. Yu Won-Jun I think his name is. People say that he has a drink problem and beats his wife but I am not surprised; seeing something like that can mess any man up…"

---

Hong-Sik approached the Yu house with Officer Ik-Kyu. Both were armed although he knew they wouldn't need their weapons. He knocked on the door and Mrs. Yu answered. "I seek your husband," he said. She gestured for them to enter. Yu Won-Jun was sitting at the table with a glass of soju in his hand.

"Why did you do it, Comrade Won-Jun?"

"Do what?"

"Murder Comrade Pak Kil-Yon."

"I didn't."

"I believe you did. You buried him in the ground and then kicked his head off. Maybe you did not do it alone but you were the instigator."

"I did do that and I don't regret doing it neither. But I never killed no Comrade Pak Kil-Yon. The man I killed was called Li Gun-Mo and he wasn't no comrade of anyone."

"He was Comrade Pak Kil-Yon."

"He may have called himself that name, but his real name was Li Gun-Mo and he was a bastard Japanese collaborator. That shit murdered my father, grandfather, uncles and brothers. He Japanese dared him to do it and he did it with a big grin on his fucking evil face. Well, now I've avenged them and so fucking arrest me, 'cos I'd do it again. My old man can sleep easy in his grave. The Yu family honour has been restored."

---

"Hello Comrade Inspector, yes, this is Captain Kang Hong-Sik in Chongpyong. I have solved the murder but I think there may be more to it than we originally thought. Can you send a telegramme or put a call through to the police in Tokyo? I want to know everything that they've got on Pak Kil-Yon and also another Japanese-Korean, Li Gun-Mo. Yes, Li Gun-Mo. Why? I'll explain all when I come over to Hamhung…"

---

It was as he'd thought. A month later when all the information on both Pak Kil-Yon and Li Gun-Mo came through, the pieces of the jigsaw slotted into place. Li Gun-Mo was a notorious figure in the Japanese underworld. He had been a collaborator and low-life during the war and had fled to Japan for fear of being attacked by relatives of his victims. In Tokyo he'd got involved in gang culture as well as drinking and gambling to excess. He had debts racked up all over the place and was known to be on the yakuza hit list. Then, two years ago, he had been found murdered, exactly three days before Pak Kil-Yon decided to migrate to Korea. The motive for the murder had been clear – the gambling debts – but what had confused the Japanese police had been the fact that he had been hanged, very irregular for the yakuza, and that none of them admittedly responsibility. Plus, when one fellow criminal had come to identify the body, he'd expressed doubts that it was Li Gun-Mo. It's very similar but I don't think it's him, the man had said.

And both Pak Kil-Yon and Li Gun-Mo shared an extraordinary physical resemblance.

# A year later

Captain Kang Hong-Sik leaned back in the chair outside his office and took a long drag of his cigarette. This was his favourite time of the day, that magical hour when the working day began to draw to a close. His eyes skirted over the scene before him: red-neckerchief-clad children returning from school; old Mun Ye-Bong guiding his equally ancient bullock and cart along the road; the grain growing lush and green in the fields, the heads blowing in the breeze while every so often a bent back betrayed the presence of a farmworker; the co-operative's little red tractor chugging along the lane; the pine-forested slopes beyond; the clear blue sky above and, in the distance, the large mosaic picture of the President depicting him inspecting a bountiful harvest. All was as it should be, all was good, all was well in the little town of Chongpyong.

He took another drag and then stood up and walked into his office. On the wall were two commendations. The first was from the Police Department of Mitaka-chu, Toyko, Japan thanking Captain Kang Hong-Sik of the Police Force of the Democratic People's Republic of Korea for his work in solving the murders of Pak Kil-Yon and Li Gun-Mo. Secretly, inwardly, Hong-Sik was proud of that commendation, although he never mentioned the fact to anyone. After all, it had been awarded by a decadent foreign power, a country that had once subjugated his homeland.

Of the second commendation however, he had no such reservations. That was for the same work but instead was awarded by his own government and people. And, at the bottom, was the signature of no less a personage than the General Himself.

And what greater honour was there on earth than that?

Hong-Sik glanced up at the picture of the General on the wall and smiled. Yes indeed, all was well in Chongpyong. All was good, all was as it should be.

**Written 15th September, 2017, Beijing-Istanbul**

# Wanna Play?

'Wanna play?'

Seitarou looked up from his comic. Who said that? There was no one there, just.

'Wanna play?'

The voice again. A small, high, metallic voice.

The speaker was tiny, perhaps 25cm high. A robot, there on the tatami mat. With a square pink body and silver arms. Its face had an anime look to it.

'Wanna play?'

'Play what?'

'A game. There's a prize at the end.'

'What prize?'

'That's up to you.'

'Up to me?'

'What do you desire most in the world?'

Seitarou thought. At school he was not popular. He had his friends but most of the kids called him a geek. All the girls did. But there was one girl, Yoshimi, who was nice sometimes. She was wonderful, like Tsukino Usagi out of Sailor Moon. What did he desire most in the world?

'There's this girl in school...'

'Let's play then!'

---

In an instant the world dissolved. Reality disappeared and digital took its place. 'Choose your weapon,' said the robot. Options appeared before him: Zanpakuto, Reverse Blade Sword, Scissor Blade... Seitarou chose the Cerberus handgun from Gungrave. He somehow knew its devastating punch and ability to allow the player to run headlong into danger would come in useful.

Weapon chosen, the game began. A forest materialised before him. A forest of bright and surreal colours. Mushrooms and rabbits jumped up. He shot them and when he hit, numbers floated up into the air. In the corner of his view he could see a score steadily increasing. His score. But he had to be careful. Squirrels lobbed nuts at him and wolves pounced. And if one struck him, he lost a life. He glanced down at the counter at the bottom. Two lost already, only seven to go. Uh-oh! But lying on the ground, were treasure chests. If he opened one he either got a life, more ammo or extra points. Life became a desperate search for treasure chests whilst missing nuts and shooting mushrooms. It was hard but in the end he passed through. 'Level Complete!' appeared before him in bold, digital letters, after he'd battled and destroyed the big bad wolf at the end. And he still had six lives left! Seitarou felt good.

---

The trolley rattled as it sped down the corridor.

'It's meningitis, these next few hours are crucial.'

'But he'll make it?'

'We'll do our best.'

---

He was in a city. A ruined city that had just endured a nuclear apocalypse. The monsters here were uglier and more dangerous. There were zombies behind the broken window panes and mutant dogs that could leap several metres. And there were alien invaders who fired back at you.

Sweat streamed from his brow and his breathing was heavy. He ran into danger and delivered deluge after deluge of bullets from his Cerberus. But whatever he did, it was not enough. Although his score kept rising to ever-dizzier heights, when he glanced down at his life counter, he was on four. He needed something extra. 'Help me!' he muttered.

In an instant the game froze and all around him was black. The pink robot was there at his feet. 'Who do you want to help you?'

'My mate Nobu,' he replied.

A pixelated version of Nobu appeared before him. But this was no normal Nobu, third-year student of Okubo Middle School. No, this was a triumphant Nobu, dressed as Goku from Dragonball.

'Help me!' he pleaded.

'I can give you one gift,' replied heroic Nobu. 'I've assessed your needs, Sei-chan, and to me what you require is greater firepower. Nothing will help you more than these.'

A flash of light emitted from his body and flew towards Seitarou. Blinded, he closed his eyes. When he opened them again, he saw that his left arm had been replaced by a bionic arm cannon that could fire energy blasts. He recognised it immediately; Astro Boy used the same weapon. Nobu loved Astro Boy.

'Are you ready to restart?' asked the robot.

Seitarou nodded.

---

By the bed in the hospital, Kawamura Nobu sat holding his friend's hand. 'Sei-chan, you fight 'em, fight them germs and diseases. We've got so much to do. You haven't even began Evangelion IV, nor did I show you my new Astro Boy manga. He uses his arm cannons to defeat the enemy. Come on mate, you can do it!'

---

With the addition of his arm cannon, he'd breezed through the remainder of the previous level. Bang! Bang! Boom! Blast! Zombies disintegrating, aliens exploding, swoosh, swish, bonus points! His score was now in seven figures but his lives were still stuck on four. Nonetheless, he survived to battle the Emperor Alien at the close, an immense, incredibly ugly being, twenty metres high and dripping with slime. Pow! Pow! Pow! Each blast of the arm cannon weakened it, but did not destroy it. So, he aimed his Cerberus at the eyes. Zap! Unable to see, the monster floundered and flailed. Then he knew that he'd won, although two swipes caught him off-guard causing the life counter to drop further. But it was enough. One final blast to the head and ka-boom! He was gone and the magical 'Level Complete' hovered in the air.

And for this new level, he had his lives restored. But the level itself, the final one according to his robot friend, was not what he'd anticipated at all. He'd expected an intergalactic spaceship, or perhaps a fantasy planet or even an evil funfair. But no, instead he found himself in his bedroom. A digitised, pixelated version of his bedroom maybe, but his own home nonetheless. Mystified, he turned to the robot who had conveniently appeared at his feet. 'It is simple,' it said, 'you simply have to walk to school to collect the girl. She is waiting for you there.'

Seitarou nodded and the robot vanished.

---

At first it was easy. There was a zombie waiting for him in the kitchen and a rabid wolf in the garden but the Cerberus saw to them. Afterwards though, it got harder. Shoppers and strollers gone berserk, pensioners with Uzis and psychotic schoolchildren thronged the roads, all trying to prevent him from reaching his goal.

But it was too much. They kept coming, the shots whizzing and whistling by his head – Ping! Pow! Zap! Individually he could deal with them, groups he could annihilate but their attacks and shots at him, the sheer volume of lead being pumped in his direction was simply too much. Although he progressed slowly – down his street, across the park, over the river (now full of mutant fish) – his life counter was dropping: four, three, two, one. Still a good kilometre from his goal, he knew that one life was not enough, even if he did chance upon a helpful treasure chest. He had lost, after coming so far, he had failed. The game was up. He was so upset he wanted a hug, some consolation and human warmth. 'Mum, I need my mum!' he sobbed.

At one the game froze and in his eye line appeared the robot. "You need your mum?" it said. 'No problem, she is here!' And then a digital mum appeared before him. She was as beautiful as his mum always had been but, being digital, she couldn't hug him. Still, having her there was some comfort.

'Mum, I failed,' he whimpered.

As if she hadn't heard him, his digital mum replied, 'Here you are Sei-chan, I've bought you a present!'

And she handed him a DVD. Evangelion IV! Nobu had seen it but he hadn't yet. Evangelion was so cool! And in IV the mechas they controlled were even better than…

Mechas… an Evangelion mecha! Yes, that was what he needed! A machine that protected him from all the flak!

And even as he thought it, the DVD transformed into a mecha itself and his mum said, 'Climb in Sei-chan, it's all yours!'

And never before had he loved her so much as at that moment.

---

Beep, beep, beep.

The heart monitor was constant at least. Seitarou's mum and dad sat by his bed, holding hands. On the iPad next to them was playing Evangelion IV which Nobu had lent them. The doctor had said that playing music or films he liked might help him. Would it? Or was the doctor just saying things like that to keep them hopeful. His mum leaned her head on her husband's shoulder and gazed across at Nobu, sitting by the bed, staring into his best friend's sleeping eyes. He was a good boy that one, a real friend. But would all this love it make a difference?

Beep, beep, beep.

Did that mean a life being restored or a life slipping away?

---

Safe inside his mecha, Seitarou blasted and stomped his way down the high street, over the railway lines and into the playground. Masses of psychotic students lunged at him, firing round after round, but he was safe. He dispatched group after group of them with his arm cannon and his score rocketed. Then he aimed at the school building itself and – Ka-boom! – ripped an enormous hole in the wall through which he strode through.

A star flashed above his classroom, indicating that was where his prize – and final challenge – lay. He tried to enter in the mecha, but it was not possible, nor too could the door be blasted. To face his final foe he would have to go in unaided. He descended from the machine and walked towards the door. It opened without him even touching it.

The classroom was empty save for the last challenge. A giant pink robot, like an oversized version of his little friend stood in the centre of the room, emotionless and uncaring. As Seitarou stepped forward it let forward a blast from its laser. Instinctively Seitarou dived behind a desk. He replied with his arm cannon and hit the mark although the damage was minimal.

For the next ten minutes, twenty minutes, hour, who knows, Sei-chan and the Evil Robot did battle. Pow! Wham! Blast! Boom! Ping! Swish! Crash! Ka-boom! It was a battle to the very end, a battle that tested every fibre of his being. Seitarou was exhausted, his body wet with perspiration, his hair matted and his limbs aching, but the robot was ailing too, the bar above its head indicating that it only had a little power left. Seitarou took aim with his arm cannon but it merely clicked. Out of ammo flashed overhead. He tried his Cerberus but that had gone ages ago. There was only a slither of life left in the beast but he had no weapon with which to finish it off. And, if he waited, the demon could rejuvenate. It was now or never. But what? Seitarou glanced down at his lives: two. Yes, that was it. Sacrifice one for the glory! He jumped out from behind the desk and ran at the machine, screaming blue murder. The robot fired a blast at him, deleting a life but before he could let loose another, Sei-chan was on his head and, with one almighty punch, he pelted the beast until the slither of life disintegrated and it fell crashing to the floor.

Sei-chan had won. Immediately before him, the door to the class storeroom opened and there stood Yoshimi. But not the Yoshimi he knew, instead a transfigured Yoshimi, like Lucy Heartfilia from Fairy Tail. She was his prize, all he had to do was collect her. He stepped forward but then stumbled. Something was wrong. He tried to get up but couldn't. He started to crawl but the energy was not there. He had won so surely...

The robot stood up from the floor, mended and well. It walked over to Seitarou, bent down and picked up the helpless child. Then, cradling him in its arms, the pink robot carried him into a brilliant light.

---

Yoshimi walked away from the funeral sad. Sei-chan had been in her class; a nice boy, he had helped her with her classwork when they'd been paired together and he'd always smiled at her. Never would he smile at her again. She sat down on one of the benches near the temple and watched the leaves of the trees rustle.

'Wanna play?'

Who was that? There's no one there.

'Wanna play?'

The voice again. A small, high, metallic voice.

Down at her feet was a little pink robot.

*Written 28th September, 2017, Stoke-on-Trent – Liverpool Lime Street – Stoke-on-Trent, UK*

# Dance Me to the End of Love

*'Dance me to the children who are asking to be born*
*Dance me through the curtains that our kisses have outworn*
*Raise a tent of shelter now, though every thread is torn*
*Dance me to the end of love'*

**Leonard Cohen**

She did not recognise the stamp on the envelope that dropped through her letterbox that Thursday afternoon, but she did recognise the handwriting. Handwriting. Who receives a handwritten letter these days? Still she knew it in an instant, even though it had been... how many years? She glanced at her husband sitting in the kitchen as she opened it, feeling guilty, as if she were committing a crime. Inside were three pieces of paper. The first was a business class plane ticket, the second a hotel reservation and the third a short note.

*Please come. I would not ask unless I had to.*

*L*

---

She exited the station with her small travel bag and sniffed the air, that chilly mixture of car fumes and alien cuisine. She had come back, back to the place where she'd spent her youth. Of course, this was far from being the first time that she'd returned since she'd left all those years ago, but this was the first time that she had come *back* and so it felt different. With him it always would.

She trod the snow-spattered streets beneath the naked lights of the streetlamps and listened to a tram rattle past. People passed her by huddled up in their winter coats and hats. She drew hers even closer around her, as if she needed some sort of extra protection against the world.

Explaining to her husband had been easy. "I have a friend back home. She is ill. I feel like I should..."

"Go," he'd said to her with a smile. "You should go; she'll appreciate it."

"But..."

"No buts, just go. Friends are important."

Friends are important. That was true. But some matter more than others.

Why did she not feel guilty for lying to him?

---

The Hotel Pugetow was easy to find. She presented her reservation to the receptionist and was surprised when she handed her the key and said, "That is a single suite for you, madam, and also a message attached from the person who booked the room. It says that you have a table reserved at the Restaurant Pod Wawelem this evening at eight. Now, if there is anything else you require, please ask."

"My friend, the gentleman who made the reservation. Is he staying here also?"

"No madam, he has not booked into this hotel. The only reservation was for yourself."

She took the lift up to the room and opened the door. It was lovely. The Pugetow was one of the new breed of boutique hotels that had sprung up all over the country. This one was especially homey with lots of personal touches. She liked that but then, she reflected, he'd known she would.

---

The Pod Wawelem hadn't changed. In half a lifetime, it was instantly recognisable, its low brick arches lined with tables accommodating diners, whilst at the end a string quartet played. All that was different now were that the spirals of cigarette smoke ascending to the barrelled ceiling had now gone, victims of the anti-smoking purges of our times.

She gave her name to the waiter and was chaperoned to a small table at the far end of the establishment. The table was adorned with fine white linen and a sprig of roses but she noticed neither. Instead she saw only him. Time had taken its toll on his features; he was grey now and aged, but it was unmistakably him. Dressed in a dark suit, a carnation in the pocket, he was as dapper as he had been then. He rose as she approached and embraced her on both cheeks. Then, upon seating her and himself, with a tear in his eye, he said, "I was afraid you wouldn't come."

She smiled and put a hand on his. "How long?" she asked.

"The doctors say a year, two maximum."

"I'm sorry to hear that."

"I've had a good life; I cannot complain."

They ate and they talked. They caught up on two separate lives that could, once upon a time, have become one. They laughed and they cried and then, when they had both finished and a bottle of wine coursed through their veins, he nodded towards the string quartet and then held out his hand.

And she put hers in his and they rose.

The quartet played an old waltz that she had not heard for almost half a century and he led her around the dark dancefloor of the restaurant. They did not speak but a thousand words were said; words of hearths never to be shared, of children never to be born, of lives that never would be, of a different future that was now the past and would always remain so.

And as the music played she rested her head on his shoulder, closed her eyes and let the music carry them away. And all that never to be became real and, for the duration of a song period, it actually happened. The life that they never led blossomed joyously in their hearts and, immune to the world that surrounded them, they danced until the end of love.

**Written 5th October, Stoke-on-Trent to Carlisle, UK**

# St. Pancras

"What's your name?"

I look at her blankly. As I have done at the thousands of others who have asked me the same question.

"You know my name already."

She looks puzzled, mixed with dashes of fear and pity. In that order.

"My name is all around you," I say by way of explanation.

She looks up, down and around, taking in shops, commuters, platforms, trains bound for Brussels, iron struts and brick walls, but the confusion remains.

*Though seeing, they do not see.*

She smiles as if that will help.

Therefore I speak in parables.

"My name is not important, madam."

I begin to play another verse, my fingers caressing the ivories with joy.

*pray and praise Thee without ceasing,*
*glory in Thy perfect love.*

*Hearing, they do not hear or understand.*

"You play well, young man."

"Thank you."

"Would you like a coffee maybe, or a sandwich?"

"No, I am alright, madam, thank you all the same."

"Do you need any other help? Where shall you sleep tonight?"

"Why, at home, madam."

"And where is home?"

"Here of course!"

"What, here in the railway station?"

"Well, where else?"

I conclude *Love Divine* and begin on *Guide Me O Thou Great Redeemer* as she digests this piece of information.

"But a young man your age needs a better home than that."

"Where could be better than here? Do you know they spent almost £800 million on this station when they refurbished it all?"

"I didn't know that, but even so, it is no place for a young boy like yourself. How old are you?"

I smile and tinkle through the chorus with a flourish. "I am one thousand, seven hundred and twenty-seven years old exactly."

"Come on, don't be silly. Why, you can't be a day over fourteen!"

"If that's what you wish to think, then I'm fine by it!"

"Really, be serious. You should be in school."

"I'm sorry, but that's not possible. I have a far more important job to do here."

"And what is that?"

"Why, bringing joy to people with my piano playing! Helping them to see that this world is not such a dark place after all, that the glory of God shines all around them, if only they would open their eyes and see it."

"I'm sorry, but I'm not a religious person, but I am worried for your safety."

"But does my music make you happy?"

"Oh yes, it's very beautiful."

"Well then, perhaps you do believe a little. To believe is to see beauty and you can do that."

I smile at her and she smiles back. She likes that, even if it does not sit well with the atheism of her upbringing.

"Well, I am concerned for you and I shall try to find you some support," she decides after involuntarily immersing herself in an entire verse.

"And I thank you for your concern," I reply.

She departs and I silently bless her. She will probably return; the good souls generally do. But she is not the one whom I am thinking of, not the one who I am playing for.

*I tell you that in the same way there will be more rejoicing in heaven over one sinner who repents than over ninety-nine righteous persons who do not need to repent.*

There he is, the lost sheep.

Sitting over there on the bench, bag at his side, head bowed, face crumpled. Ten minutes ago he contemplated the ultimate act; his debt, his unfaithful lover, his bullying boss and his ill mother all stabbing at his soul till it could take no more. He was walking through here on his way to the Thameslink platforms to do it. There are trains every few minutes in that dark tunnel.

I understand. I remember vividly that day, the sun blazing overhead, when I was led out amidst the jeering masses towards that axe wielded by a masked servant of the authorities. There was no hope, no way out, no way forward. At that moment, face-to-face with death, one feels truly alone.

*My God, my God, why hast thou forsaken me?*

But then he heard my chords, the harmony of note caressing note, the joy that a piano can bring. He stopped. He mouthed silently words unsung since childhood.

> *Jesus, Thou art all compassion;*
> *pure unbounded love Thou art;*
> *visit us with Thy salvation;*
> *enter ev'ry trembling heart.*

And now he sits, danger passed, contemplating life, not death.

I finish my song and he looks up. I smile at him and he smiles back.

My job is done.

Do you honestly think that, if you name a station St. Pancras, then its protector will not bother to dwell under its great iron roof?

*Written 16th October, 2017, Birmingham, UK*

# Victoria Falls

A vast space, floor tiles so clean that you can eat your dinner off them. People bustling here and there, suits, tracksuits, t-shirts, hijabs. The whole of humanity in a rush, London on the move.

He looks up. *Due: 17:50 Destination: Brighton, Status: Expected17:52 2 mins late, Platform: 15; Due: 17:52 Destination: Ashford International via Maidstone East, Status: On time, Platform: 1…*

Brighton, Ashford, Epsom, Orpington, Dorking, Surrey: he's never been to any of those places, nor will he ever go. Nineteen years old and he knows that he will never see Orpington either via Herne Hill or any other route.

A thought crashes through his mind. He'll abandon all of this and jump on the blue and white Southeastern train to Orpington via Herne Hill.

What is that hill like he wonders; is it tall and steep or low and flat? Are there houses there or is it like the mountains around Mirpur where his gran's house is?

Orpington disappears from his mind just as it disappears from the departures board and is replaced by the image of his smiling, kindly, wrinkled grandmother serving up nihari for breakfast. The smell is magical, the marrow bone covered in the rich sauce, chapattis at the side to soak up the rich juices. Oh, to eat that one more time, to…

He puts those thoughts out of his mind with a prayer. Thoughts like that come from one place only and their purpose is to distract, to confuse the believer. But he is not to be distracted; he has but one purpose. He looks up at the clock. *17:54.* Not long now. He stares and stares, willing for the four to become a five. Then it flicks over and he presses.

*Astaghfirullah, ting is man it's da caliphate innit, caliphate's da way forward cos dat's Allah's plan see cos that's how it's outlined in the Quran and in them early days when the Prophet (peace be upon him) was ruling in Mecca and that everythin was perfect, everythin worked but now as the kufur's in control and that we've got wars an people dyin and everythin cos its all about Allah an Allah is bein disrespected an that so we need to get da caliphate back akhi we need da caliph who is da descendent of the Prophet (peace be upon him) an all will be fine den, Alhamdulillah, it will be beautiful akhi peace and everyfin wiv justice for everyone even the kufur cos that is Allah's will see. But no caliphate is gonna come about jus cos we want it, no way bruv, dat ain't happenin even if it is Allah's will no it's a test akhi a test from Allah on us, da belivers da Ummah to see if we're deserving of it which is why obviously da ting has to be done.*

Can you hear yourself? Do you know just how ridiculous you sound? Arabic exhortations mixed in with some faux Jamaican slang and a load of political claptrap that you don't understand. Don't you know that the prophet never even instituted the caliphate, that came after his death when they started fighting over who should take the spoils of his victories. And do you also know that three of the first four caliphs was murdered before his time? That hardly sounds like the recipe for political stability now, does it? Come on, just stop a minute and listen to yourself! You're brainwashed, man, brainwashed!

*And you bruv is being disrespectful to the Prophet (peace be upon him) and the deen bruv, an da deen man you's like some sort of apostate an you know what should happen to dem death akhi death as it sez in da Quran word of Allah.*

Death, eh? Why bother? Close enough as it is sitting here in this fucking room that stinks of Domestos, doors slamming shut, keys being turned in locks, madmen shouting, bells ringing, staring into the eternal blackness and having to listen to you all day. Death sounds fun compared to that. And besides, isn't death what you want so much anyway? First it's a reward and then it's a punishment. Make your mind up won't you or, oh no, wait a minute, I forgot, you gave that up when you let the Brothers start telling you what to think all the time.

*Astaghfirullah now you turn to da brevren dem blessed soldiers of Allah who know and live da truth and you is sayin day I'm da one dat is brainwashed but maybe bruv it is you dat is brainwashed by da kufur and dere kufur ways like you is some sort a coconut brown on the outside but white on da inside innit but I ain't no coconut an I never will be an the only fing dat guides me is Islam Maa shaa Allah.*

You'll never be a coconut, eh? A kind of contradiction if ever I heard one. Whatever; you still haven't explained how you going to that station is going to bring about the caliphate or how you getting blown to smithereens by your handmade bag of nails is any different to me being shot now because you reckon that I'm an apostate despite the fact that I pray five times a day, attend Jumma every week and keep Allah in my heart.

*Man, martyrdom is martyrdom and normal death is normal death innit, Astaghfirullah one is all paradise wiv seventy fit as fuck virgins and da other is eternal hellfire for da sin of shirk simple akhi noffin else to say an when I do detonate that bomb I shall immediately wivout delay be up dere wiv dem virgins and in a garden of such beauty an dat dat you cannot even imagine it whereas you bruv you will still be sat dere wiv your half a beard gazing into space like some spaz or summit wonderin where it all went wrong.*

Wondering where it all went wrong. Yeah, I can agree with you on that one. Where did it all go wrong…? Get out man, get out! Before you came I was ok, lost in my thoughts and now… fuck, you always do this to me! Leave you bastard!

*Leave? I ain't leavin nowhere akhi an don't expect me ta start feelin for you an that just cos there's a tear drippin from your eye cos I am your conscious bruv I am da reminder from da Almighty so as you cant forget I am da pure soul see.*

You make me laugh. You couldn't even spell pure.

*I am da one bruv dat has da courage to put on his jacket wiv da detonator inside I am da true believer and you is da coconut kuffur unbeliever simple innit akhi I is da one who will go dere an press dat button an shout Allahu Akbar so dey know dat did is da caliphate callin an den…*

Then…

… then what?

Victoria falls?

Boom?

Fucking idiot! Fucking brainwashed, too young, too immature, too naïve little, lovable, misguided idiot!

You've gone now I see; you always leave at this point.

---

Boom! Bright lights! Darkness! Complete, absolute darkness. Ya Allah! Protect me!

Silence.

---

I love you and I hate you. I understand you and yet you are alien to me. You were so young, so full of anger at the injustices you saw and so full of a desire to change the world for the better.

Yet what did you know of that world you wished to change beyond the streaked grey concrete, mobile repairs shop infested, kebab house blessed, burqa wearing, OFSTED failing confines of Tower Hamlets?

Or the harsh mountains of Kashmir where your father took you every few years when he managed to save up enough money?

You didn't know so the brothers taught you. Those jovial, welcoming, wise men with beards who had an answer for every problem.

Who melted away into the mist when you'd done there bidding.

Who ran out of wisdom when you ended up blind, wheelchair-bound and in pain in here.

In short, when you became me.

Astaghfirullah.

---

He fell in October 2018, on a day that was so still and quiet in the news that the newspapers headlined with a story about Tanzania. He didn't make the inner pages. After all, who was he? Mohammed Safdar was nothing but an impressionable young man who, fifteen years earlier had tried to detonate a homemade bomb in Victoria station.

The bomb, as was reported at the time, had not exploded properly and the only person hurt was himself. He'd spent the last decade and a half in Broadmoor, unable to see, unable to walk, talking to the people in his head caused by the schizophrenia brought on by trauma.

He was found in his cell. He had sunk forwards and was lying on the ground as if asleep. When they turned him over his face wore an expression that was so composed that it looked as if he were almost happy that it had turned out that way.

*Written xxxx*

# Day Off

It was the cold that woke him that morning. There had been an unusually chilly snap for the previous two days yet he'd not remembered to adjust the heating to compensate and instead merely thrown another duvet onto the bed. Yet sometime during the night it had slipped off.

Automatically he retrieved it from the floor, laid it over the other and then snuggled back inside. He had been in the middle of a dream about Anna. They had been lying on the bed together, his hand stroking her perfect, smooth body. Why had his mind turned to her? That had been, what, forty years before? Half a lifetime. And it had never really been anything anyway. He'd known from the outset that it could never work between the two of them; they just weren't suited. She was too much of a princess for starters. As he thought that thought, he chastised himself silently. Princess. The word sounded cheap, like some spoilt bimbo with too much make-up. Anna was nothing of the sort. She was a princess in that she was regal. She was the most supremely elegant person he had ever encountered. The way she walked, the way she moved her hands, the way she smiled... a born royal.

A born royal whom he had met in takeaway.

As he recalled Anna, another thought crashed into his head. How come the cold had woken him and not his alarm? Had he forgotten to set it? What time was it? Was he late? Where was he even meant to be that day? A meeting in Leiden perhaps or...

Then he remembered. There was no meeting and he had set no alarm. It was his day off. The day his boss had forced him to take off. There was two months until the new financial year and he still had most of his holidays outstanding. So, he'd agreed to every Thursday as leave until the start of April.

A whole day off, but what would he do with it? In this cold what could anyone do. He snuggled further under the covers and tried to recall Anna's body next to his but she had faded. So too had any desire to sleep. Reluctantly he rose.

---

Sitting in his kitchen eating breakfast, he mused that it was rather pleasant to be able to savour his coffee and toast. Many days he skipped them altogether, or grabbed something on the way. That satisfied his hunger but left his soul wanting. A meal should be enjoying whilst still in both mind and body. He looked out of the window and fixed his eyes on a bird perched on a fencepost singing its heart out. He watched that bird for a full minute before it flew away. Then he poured himself a second coffee and picked up his paperback, savouring a full chapter of unsolved murder in Malmo before the cup was drained.

But he could not relax completely. Out of the corner of his left eye he spied the unwashed dishes from yesterday and the unwashed clothes from last week.

And out of his right eye he caught site of the fence that still needed repairing.

So that was to be his destiny: a full day of washing, mending, tidying...

A twinge across his chest caught him by surprise. Digestion probably, yet such passing pains worried him. He was no longer young. As he thought on this he noticed the ache in his right knee. That had never been right since his accident three years before. And the tablets waiting on the table before him reminded him of something else: the harsh words of Dr. Souterdijk during his last appointment. Those commandments issued with medical authority: destress, work less, exercise more. "But it is hard!" he had pointed out.

"A stroke is harder," Souterdijk had replied.

He swallowed the tablets in one gulp and felt a sudden urge to get away.

But to where?

---

He bought a ticket to Nijmegen. He decided on the spot. He had approached the ticket machine, scanned through the names listed alphabetically and Nijmegen had jumped out at him. He couldn't say why, it just did. He had been before, back when he was a student. Forty years ago. Half a lifetime.

The train went via Centraal. As they departed another train, an identical yellow and blue tube, ran beside them on a parallel track. For some reason it made him think of Anna again. Why was he thinking of her so much today? What had caused him to dream about her? It was not as if they could have ever been anything. They were just too different. But back then, at that period in his life, she was what he'd needed. Anna hadn't just been elegant, she was also an excellent listener. And he'd needed that. Plus, she'd needed him too; a friend with a shoulder on which she could lay her head; an oasis of stability in a desert of turmoil. He'd thought at the time that her name was apt. He read a lot of Russian literature back then and she was just like the chaotic, half-mad yet addictive Anna Karenina. And for a while they'd been happy, walking hand-in-hand through life, like these two trains travelling side-by-side.

The other train swerved off north towards Gronigen.

Their lives had diverged too.

---

There was a smattering of snow on the fields and red-roofed houses as they passed through the countryside. In the spring these were the famous bulb fields, a riot of colour attracting coachloads of pensioners from Dusseldorf to Dijon. Now though, it was all a dreary, grey.

Beyond the naked fields a line of white windmills thwap-thwapped in the wintry wind. They made him feel miserable. Was that what he was like? One of a line, working mindlessly, automatically come wind or shine, thwap-thwapping his way through the days, repaired by Dr. Souterdijk and his tablets when he could be, but when irrevocably broken and life-expired, to be thrown onto the scrap heap, entirely replaceable, a younger model in line to step in and take over.

He became aware of the dull ache in his right knee again and grimaced. Were these weekly leave days the beginning of the end for his thwap-thwapping through life? Would aimless days like this slowly become the norm rather than the exception.

He shivered.

The train passed over a lengthy iron bridge, clattering as it did so. Beneath them on the steel-grey river passed a long barge. The front end was dripping with icicles and the sailors slid about in their heavy sou'westers. The rear of the boat though was ice-free.

'Why is that?' he wondered.

---

Nijmegen's railway station was pleasant. It had cast-iron canopies dating from a more elegant time. Even as that word popped into his head, it brought Anna trailing in its wake. Wouldn't it be nice to be waiting for a train here with her, his own Anna Karenina? Then he remembered how that Anna had ended her days.

Maybe not.

For some reason the machine wouldn't recognise his ticket and he had to call the assistant.

---

The centre was only a short walk from the station. Compared to most Dutch cities, Nijmegen is quite hilly. He noticed that more than anything else, it put extra strain on his knee. The rest was much the same. The same brick buildings, the same shops on the ground floors, the same Ikea furnishings adorning those above; the same bicycles carrying citizens, the same *Nee-Ja* stickers on the letter boxes. No unaddressed advertising material; Yes door-to-door sheets.

The red man on the crossing took as long to change to green as he did back home too.

---

He dined in a vegetarian café that advertised yoga as a way to improve your life. He'd never tried yoga; perhaps it would help? He made a mental note to mention it to Dr. Souterdijk. In principle it sounded ok, but with his aching knee, would it be wise? On the next table a gay couple sat kissing. It made him feel uneasy, not because they were gay but because one man was older the him and the other clearly in his twenties.

He stirred his tea and opened up his paperback but could not concentrate. Why did the age difference bother him so much? Was it a justifiable concern or was he being old-fashioned, prejudiced even? Mentally he put himself on trial. How can I be prejudiced when I don't even mind that they're gay? Why are you even casting judgements on such things; who someone loves is none of your business? But how can one person truly be close with another when that other has no life experience? What do you know anyway; where's your great track record of relationship success?

The gay men left holding hands and the jury adjourned to make a decision.
But then his lunch arrived and the jury forgot to return.

---

The museum in the Grote Markt was closed, as too the great church of St. Stephen. He went down to the riverside which he recalled as being nice from his student days visit. Back then he would head off once or twice a week on the train to some random town, usually with Koen, but on occasions Piet, Anna, Gaab or Anneke. People joked that he was like an old man since he loved to amble around, drinking in coffeeshops and watching the world go by. He'd loved it though.

The riverside was nice but it was cold. In the summer it would be a great place to sit and drink coffee but now the wind whipped against his cheeks. He mused with a smile that back then he'd been compared to an old man yet these days, when he truly was old, this was the first time he'd wandered around a town aimlessly in years. Now life was frantic and relentless and he struggled to keep up with it. A barge passed by on the river. That too had ice encrusting the front but the rear was free. Was it because the front charged into the wind which created an extra chill factor? Koen would have known that; he'd studied Physics.

He missed Koen.

---

Waiting on the railway station was a young lady wearing a faceveil. When his train pulled in she boarded and sat across the carriage from him. He was shocked to see that the skin around her blue eyes was pale. She must be a convert! What on earth would cause a young Dutch girl to convert to Islam and wear something like that? Why would you give up so much freedom?

Again, he felt a voice inside his head remonstrating him. The case was resumed, the jury were back in court: So, what if she converted, you're not religious anyway, why should you care? Who is to say that Islam is backward, that she has no freedom? Come on though, look at her: it hardly says 'liberated' now, does it? She must have done it for a man and is it right that someone should convert to be with the one they love? Is that love when you have to give up part of yourself? How can you say that; you don't even know if she did it for a man or if she chose it freely?

He kept glancing at her, she fascinated him. He longed to ask her about her life and the choice that she had made but he knew that it would only come across weird. He couldn't see her face now as she was looking out of the window at the frost-laden world beyond, but his eyes fixed on her pale hands. They were elegant hands, like Anna's had been. Anna had blue eyes like this girl too. Could he have imagined Anna converting to Islam and wearing a veil? He closed his eyes and tried to imagine it.

He was jerked back to reality by the announcement of the next stop. The veiled girl rose without looking at him and got off. He was alone.

Back in the house he took a pizza from the freezer and put it in the oven. Then he took a beer to accompany it and settled down in front of the TV. The news was all about the cold weather and a crash on the A15 involving ten vehicles that had slipped on the ice. A reporter was on the scene talking about casualties and types of tyre but it could not hold his interest. Instead his mind drifted back to Anna again. Why was she on his mind so much today, that fleeting relationship from four decades before?

He switched off the TV and questioned why he had never looked her up, tried to get in touch. It wasn't as if they had parted under a cloud after all.
He then wondered what she was doing and where she lived these days. Thoughts crashed around his head and disquieted him. Was that why he had had that dream? To seek her out?

He removed his laptop from its case and set it on the kitchen table. He typed her name in, knowing that it would reveal nothing; she'd be married now and living under a different surname.

Yet to his surprise he got a result first time. She was even friends with a couple of his friends from Facebook. He clicked on the page. Yes, that was her, definitely. Older, true, yet still regal and refined. He gazed into those deep blue eyes. Did he ever occupy her mind like she had done his today? He scanned down. She had wished her granddaughter a happy sixth birthday last week.

The granddaughter was named Klara.

He gazed at her picture for a very long time, whilst the cursor hovered over the *Add Friend* button.

Then he remembered that he had a seminar in Rotterdam the following morning to prepare for.

*Written 02/03/18, Arnhem, Netherlands*

# No New Messages, No Missed Calls

She puts on her make-up. Foundation, more foundation. Blusher, mix it in. cover up all those spots, those imperfection, that horrible skin. Make something presentable out of that plain face. Do the eyebrows, carefully with the liner, make them beautiful... somehow. It is complete... or at least, as good as it can be. It is a mask. Protection against the world.

They say she is pretty. They tell her repeatedly. But she doesn't really believe it. The mirror doesn't lie. She is prettier than that fat thing Emily she knows, no doubt, but that's not hard. And how can she truly be beautiful with such horrible skin, big shoulders, lank hair... Prettier than Emily is no compliment. How big must she be? A hundred kilos maybe? Why are so many of the local girls so big? It is probably the food they eat she decides, all those kebabs, pizzas and chips. Gypsies are fat too. Here they lump her together with Roza who is not so much smaller than Emily. Yet there is a world of difference between them. Back home she would never even talk to a gypsy, let alone hang out with her. But here... what choice is there?

She walks out. The air is chilly but she doesn't mind particularly. There are seagulls overhead. They caw continually. She leaves her road and walks down the hill to the High Street. She stops in the grey street and sits on one of the seats put there for old and homeless people. She watches the gulls swoop and swirl, cawing all the while, looping and cawing, up and down, riding the wind and then diving down when they spy a morsel of food. She takes her bag from her side, puts it on her lap and opens it. She takes out her phone and checks it. No new messages, no missed calls. She puts it back and from inside the bag she takes out a chocolate bar. Crunchie. It was one of the first English words that she learned. 'C-r-oo-n-ch-i-e.' Later though she found out that she'd been saying it wrong; there was no 'e' on the end even though they wrote it, and the 'oo' was more like an 'a'. But she still likes the taste; there is nothing like it back home. She breaks off a few crumbs and throws them for the birds. They swoop down and carry them off in their beaks.

She gets up and leaves. She wanders the half-empty streets past shops both open and boarded-up. After some time, she reaches the sea and it reminds her of when they first arrived here. She had been so excited by the sea; the sea meant holidays! Now though, it seems so normal. The sea here is grey and dull, like a sheet of unpainted metal. There are lots of ships on it today as every day. Where are they going? Which strange lands did they come from? What exciting cargo do they carry in all those containers? Sometimes, on clear days, she can see the coast of France beyond them. Not today though; there is too much cloud. She still stares out there, trying to discern the lumps of hills. Why not? What better is there to do? She takes her phone out of her bag and looks at it. No new messages, no missed calls. She puts it back and sits and stares out to sea.

The chilly wind gets to her eventually, breaking through the barrier of her puffed-up coat and causing her to shiver. She gets up and returns to the town. As she walks down the street she spies Mark and Ethan coming up it in the opposite direction. She darts down a side road and then into an alley until they have passed. They are both total idiots, "dickheads" the other girls in her class call them. She doesn't want to have to talk to them. Ethan is leery too. He once told her that she had a "cute arse". She'd had to ask Emily later what that meant. The thought of going with him – yuck!

They pass and she resumes her journey. She walks down street after street with no particular destination or direction. In the middle of one there is an empty Fanta can. She kicks it and a car comes down a few seconds later and runs over it. Crunch!

Like Crunchie.

She reaches the playground by the flats. There are no seagulls here for some reason, only sparrows. No kids either. They must all be in school or nursery. She sits on the swing and swings herself up and down remembering when she was a kid and used to love going to the playground. Her dad would push her and she would rise and then fall, rise and then fall, rise and then fall...

Drops of rain on her face shake her from her memories. Why is it always raining in England? She runs for the shelter and then sits on the wooden bench inside watching the rain pour down. As she watches, she opens her bag and takes out her phone. No new messages, no missed calls. She takes out the second Crunchie and realises that she is hungry. She unwraps it carefully and then eats it in exactly five bites.

Why is she here she wonders to herself. She never asked to come, never chose this life. Why here? Why me? She glances down at her arm, pulls her sleeve up and winces. She pulls the sleeve back down again quickly and spies the final Crunchie in her bag. Why not? She eats this one in seven bites and doesn't enjoy it as much as the last one.

She notices that the sky has started to darken and thinks she felt her phone vibrate. She take it out. 10,000 steps completed today. No new messages, no missed calls.

The rain has stopped. She leaves.

She walks the long way home but the phone never rings nor vibrates.

As she turns the key and enters through the door, she learns that her mum is back already; the smell of cooking gives her presence away. "Claudia, is that you?" mum calls.

"Yeah."

"How was school?"

"Ok."

"Did you take those three chocolate bars from the fridge?"

"The Crunchie bars?"

"Yeah, those ones.

"I took them. I ate them in my breaks."

"Oh Claudia, I really wish you would eat more healthily."

She glanced at her phone.

No new messages, no missed calls.

*Inspired by a visit to NACRO Dover, 13/03/18*
*Mapped out 13/03/18 Dover Priory to London St. Pancras, UK*
*Written 14/03/18, Hampton Hotel, Birmingham, UK*

# Death in Paradise

*There was a merchant in Bagdad who sent his servant to market to buy provisions and in a little while the servant came back, white and trembling, and said, Master, just now when I was in the marketplace I was jostled by a woman in the crowd and when I turned I saw it was Death that jostled me. She looked at me and made a threatening gesture, now, lend me your horse, and I will ride away from this city and avoid my fate. I will go to Samarra and there Death will not find me. The merchant lent him his horse, and the servant mounted it, and he dug his spurs in its flanks and as fast as the horse could gallop he went. Then the merchant went down to the marketplace and he saw me standing in the crowd and he came to me and said, Why did you make a threating gesture to my servant when you saw him this morning? That was not a threatening gesture, I said, it was only a start of surprise. I was astonished to see him in Bagdad, for I had an appointment with him tonight in Samarra...*

"What are you reading, love?"

"Just a collection of short stories by a guy called Somerset. I picked it up from a charity shop in Wigan before we came out."

"Any good?"

"Yeah, I'm quite enjoying it."

"Lend it me afterwards; this thriller I've got is crap. Fancy a drink?"

"Not now; maybe later."

"Suit yourself, but I'm having a lager. Already paid for when all's said and done."

"More like you want to get a closer look at that new arrival over there."

"What new arrival?"

"Mark Botham, you can't fool me; I've been married to you for seventeen years! You know very well which one."

"And you should know that I've only ever had eyes for you Vikki Botham."

"Get away with you! Tell you what though, I will have a drink after all: a cup of tea, love, strong, just how I like it..."

---

Heads raised from their sun loungers when she walked by the pool with her luggage before checking in sometime around one o'clock in the afternoon. "I wonder who that is?" said Barbara Simpson to her husband Mick.

"I don't know, dear," he replied, "but we can find out later when she comes down to the pool."

In the reception Mercedes Garcia took down the details of the newcomer. "Ms. Maveth, yes, we have your booking here through booking.com. Four nights is it? Excellent! Enjoy your stay at the *Flamingo Beach*!"

---

An hour later Ms. Maveth had stowed away her baggage, changed into a bikini and made her way down to the pool. Lazily, she climbed into the chlorine-blue water and swam across to the pool bar. As she hoisted herself onto one of the stools, several pairs of eyes watched her intently.

"Who do we have here then?" asked Len Howell.

"Dunno, but I wouldn't mind finding out," replied his mate Dan McCluskey.

"She's kind of mysterious-looking, don't you think?" said Mark Botham.

"She could do with a tan," replied Vikki.

"Probably why she's here. How old do you reckon she is?" asked Barbara

"Hard to tell. Could be anything between twenty and fifty," replied Mick.

---

Sometime later she opened her eyes to find a figure standing over her. "Sorry to bother you but we noticed you check-in. Your first time here?"

She nodded.

"Welcome to paradise! Mick Simpson and me wife Barbara over there. We've been coming to the Flamingo Beach for years. Fancy a sangria? All paid for after all!"

"Don't mind if I do," she replied. "My name's De."

"Nice to meet you, De. We love it here! Sun, sangria and siestas, what more could you want?"

"Indeed. I'm shattered; been busy with work. I've come to recharge my batteries."

"No better place! What is it you do, by the way?"

De was about to answer when Barbara shouted over, "I could do with that sangria, dear!" Mick winked. "When the boss calls, I have to run," he said before scuttling off.

---

As she was finishing her sangria, Len sidled up. "Alright, darling, fancy me topping that up for you? All paid for."

She smiled. "Not yet."

"Aye, pacing yourself's wise. Len Howell by the way." He paused, implying that she should give her name but she said nothing and instead only stared at him. "And what's your name?" he eventually said.

"Not 'darling'," she replied, before turning over onto her front.

---

The next morning she came down wearing a different bikini. The Simpsons were already out on the loungers, getting what they had paid for. They greeted her as she passed and she smiled back. "Fancy sitting with us, De?" asked Barbara, indicating towards an empty lounger.

"Don't mind if I do," De replied.

"I'll get the sangrias!" announced Mick.

As he toddled off, Barbara bent over. "De, I was wondering, is that your real name or is it short for something?"

"Short for something."

"That makes sense; never heard of it before. What's your surname, dear?"

"Maveth."

"Maveth, now that is unusual; I've never heard that one before."

"I believe it's Jewish."

"Jewish, eh? My grandmother on my mother's side was Jewish." Barbara nodded gravely. "She came from Manchester," she added, as if that explained everything.

---

Jenny, the TUI rep came around bearing flyers. "It's karaoke night at *El Cid's* tonight," she announced. "Big prize, fifty euros."

"Cash or vouchers?" asked De.

"Vouchers of course," replied Jenny.

"But everything here is free; it's all-inclusive."

"Fifty euros off your next trip."

Mick smiled. "Barbara and I will be entering. Probably our usual *Paradise by the Dashboard Light* double-act."

"I've heard it's amazing," said Jenny, who had heard the exact opposite.

"It is. What about you, De; will you be grabbing the mic?"

"Maybe," she replied.

---

On the table by the barbeque was a folded-up copy of the *Sun*. De glanced at it as she ordered three cheeseburgers for herself and the Simpsons. Vikki Botham noticed that glance as she drew on her cigarette. "Take it, love, I've finished with it."

"No, I'm alright; they only contain bad news."

"Too right. There was a terrorist bombing again today; somewhere in Germany."

"That's awful."

"Luckily no one killed. They reckon the blast went off wrong. Made a bloody mess of the street though, look at the pictures!"

De picked it up and did look. Vikki was right; the bomb had made a right mess.

---

"Ladies and gentlemen, we have a new contender on the stage this evening. Please give a warm hand to De who's going to sing *Don't Fear the Reaper* for us." Jenny grinned widely across her über-tanned face. The contrast with the singer's pale visage and serious expression was palpable.

> *All our times have come*
> *Here but now they're gone*

"Oh, I remember this one," said Barbara. "When she said the name it didn't ring a bell, but now I've heard the tune..."

"Blue Öyster Cult, 1973; a classic," pronounced Mick.

> *Seasons don't fear the reaper*
> *Nor do the wind, the sun or the rain*

"She's got a nice pair of lungs on her," observed Dan.

"And a nice pair of something else," added Len.

"Bit weird though. Serious like."

"Still wouldn't say no."

> *Romeo and Juliet*
> *Are together in eternity*

"I spoke with her today at the barbeque," said Vikki.

"Aye? Looks a bit posh for this place."

"Not when you speak to her."

"Where's she from?"

"Never said. Not much of an accent neither."

"Be down south somewhere then."

*Come on baby,*
*Baby take my hand,*
*We'll be able to fly!*

"Well done De! Everyone, give our newcomer a warm round of *El Cid's'* applause!"

---

"Where are you from, love? I meant to ask yesterday but I forgot."

"Nowhere in particular. We moved around a lot as a kid and I still do now. My work takes me all over the place."

"That explains why you haven't got much of an accent. Do you want me paper again?"

"If you don't mind."

"Not much in it. A quiet news day. There was a crash on the M6, that's about it."

"Really? How many fatalities?"

"None actually. Lucky."

"Yes, lucky."

---

"It's De I believe…?"

"How do you know that?" The look which she gave Dan McCluskey as he sidled up to her in *El Cid's* was more one of curiosity than contempt.

"Old Ma Simpson, she knows everything."

"I'd figured that." She smiled and twisted the straw from her Sex on the Beach around her fingers. They were elegant fingers. Everything about this girl had class.

"You not singing tonight?"

"It's not karaoke on Saturdays. It's Elvis."

"And there was me thinking that Elvis was dead."

"And there was me thinking I saw him in *Lidl* last week."

"Dead or not, I'd still prefer to be listening to you. You've got a lovely pair of lungs on you, De."

"Is that all I've got?"

"Dunno, you tell me."

"Let's go find out shall we...?"

The lights dimmed and smoked filled the room. Then there was a loud, long drumroll.

"Ladies and gentlemen," announced Jenny, "I give you the King of Rock and Roll himself!"

De and Dan exited stage right.

---

"You're leaving tomorrow, aren't you dear?"

"I'm afraid so, Barbara, got to get back to work."

"You never did tell me what it was that you do. Not that it matters. A shame that you're leaving though; our friends Ned and Grace are coming."

"Your friends holiday in the same place?"

"Of yes, of course; we met them here, fifteen years ago. They come regularly just like us. We always get our times to match up."

"Perhaps I'll catch them next year instead."

"Oh, but you won't! The thing is, Ned..." At this point Barbara leant in and lowered her voice. "Ned, he's... he's not going to be with us for much longer... cancer."

She pronounced the word with a solemnity that befitted its awesomeness.

"Doctor said six months at the most," added Mick cheerfully.

---

"I heard she went with him last night."

Mark Botham closed his eyes, as if imagining it. "Who went with who?"

"Her. That one you're always gawping at and pond life over there."

"Pond life?"

"That prick from St. Helen's who can't say a sentence without putting the f-word into it."

"Dan?"

"Is that his name?"

"Yeah, I had a beer with him yesterday. And you're right, not particularly bright or charming. Still, fair play to him."

"What was that?!"

"I meant, fair play him finding someone when he's on holiday; stop him being lonely like. Not that I have that problem with you, my angel, at my side, Vikki Botham."

"Oh, get away with you, Mark Botham, and get me another cup of tea."

---

"Here we are again, back in paradise!" announced Ned, gazing up at the twenty-two floors of concrete.

"I wonder where the Simpsons are; it'll be great to catch up with them again."

"By the pool like where they always are I should imagine. Come on, old girl!"

---

"So, you actually managed to get off with her then!"

Dan and Len were sitting at the pool bar sipping pints of lager. Both were tracing their eyes over the pale figure lying on a sun lounger clad in a black one-piece swimsuit.

"Aye. Made me move in *El Cid's*, she couldn't get enough so we went back to her place and wham, bam, thank you ma'am!"

"Respect, mate. When I went up to her she was dead stand-offish."

"Obviously not her type," replied Dan, glancing up at Len's head.

Len, conscious of his bald spot, ignored the jibe. "Anyway, what were she like? I mean, she's a tidy piece to look at but a bit weird."

"Honest truth, mate, weird is the word. There were no foreplay, nowt romantic, just got down and did it. And during the act as you may call it, she just lay there, hardly moving, just... there."

"Really? Just passive like?"

"Mate, it were like fucking a corpse. And afterwards she just got up, put her clothes on and went out again for another drink. Like we'd both just been in a meeting together and now the meeting were over, it were time to move on."

"Weird. Well, I did think she looked a bit strange like."

"Yeah, almost emotionless she was, except that, well, throughout the whole time, I got the sense of power, like she possessed some sort of great power, but she were choosing not to use it."

"What made you think that?"

"In all honesty, I can't say; I just felt it. Like I said, weird."

"Aye, weird. Another beer?"

"Don't mind if I do."

In the background, De lazily turned over onto her back.

---

"Hi there!"

"Ned, Grace, you made it! And you're looking well!"

"Wish I felt so well as I look, but we're here now; couple of weeks in paradise with two old friends."

"Oh, by the way, let me introduce a new friend of ours. This is De, she's leaving tomorrow but we've had a jolly time here together."

De Maveth stood up from her lounger and took off her sunglasses. In an instant the colour drained from Ned Parkes' cheeks until he was as pale as the woman he now faced. "You!" he cried, pointing at her with a shaking finger. "What are you doing here? Not here, not now!" And then, in an instant, he turned on his heels and ran.

"What was all that about?" asked Barbara.

"Do you know him?" asked Grace.

"Never seen him before in my life," replied De.

---

## *Ten hours later*

Tick-tock, tick-tock, tick-tock.

Ned Parkes gazed at the clock on the wall of his shed. After seeing her he had run, not even bothering to collect his luggage, straight out of the Flamingo Beach, out of Benidorm, out of Spain itself, all the way back home to Rochdale. Here he was, in his own special domain, the shed at the bottom of his garden. Here he was safe.

Yet now he was here, he couldn't concentrate. His hands shook when he tried to hammer in a nail. Trying to shake his mind away from things he picked up the paper. The usual. A house-fire in Cardiff; thankfully all the occupants rescued. Another crash on the M6. No fatalities. Lucky.

Knock, knock.

Not wanting to do so, yet somehow compelled by forces beyond his control, he got up from his chair, walked across the room and opened it. There, waiting for him was Death... or 'De' for short.

"You were there... in Benidorm..." he stammered.

"A chance meeting. I was on holiday, taking a few days off. But back at work today and my first appointment is you."

"But I ran! I escaped you!"

"Ned, there is no escaping me. We were always destined to meet here at this time. You seeing me on my holiday was just a coincidence."

*Written 16th-19th April, 2018, Stoke-on-Trent – Leeds – London – Birmingham, UK*

# Victory

It was a bright cold day in April and the clocks were striking seventeen. Brendan O'Dwyer looked down at the ticket in his hand, soon to be obsolete.

*London Euston to Victory-on-Sea. Single. 13-04-1994. Inparty.*

There was a hoot on the whistle and the train began to slow. He had arrived.

The first thing that he noticed was the paint.

It was fresh. It did not peel and the colours were not faded. The initials O.S.R. were clearly picked out in gold on a maroon background. How many years had he seen a railway station looking so smart? Normally all was dirty and soot-covered. Here though, it was like those dim memories of his childhood.

He alighted from the train, his suitcase in hand and went into the smart station building. Soldiers were waiting there. He showed them both his ticket which they took and his passport which was returned to him. Then they nodded and he made his way out.

He was tired. The journey had been a long and arduous one. The express had left London at 07:14 that morning, only twenty minutes after the scheduled time, and had taken a full eight and a half hours to steam up to Carlisle – with lengthy stops in Rugby, Crewe and Preston – before an hour-long wait for the twice-daily service on to Victory-on-Sea, which took a full forty-five minutes to trundle and shake its way down the thirty-five kilometres or so of track to the coast. And so, a full ten hours or more after starting his journey, with the sky already beginning to darken, he had arrived.

There were a dozen or so other travellers that the train had disgorged. All were led onto the horse-drawn bus that was waiting outside with

'Victory-on-Sea Transport' emblazoned on its side. Their names were taken, the driver tugged on the reins and they were off. They rumbled along wide, clean streets lined with elegant hotels from the Pre-Revolutionary Era. To his right, just visible, was the front, the dark waters of the Solway Firth and then the Scottish hills beyond, but between the road and the beach an elegant park with well-tended lawns, a bandstand and benches upon which people sat. all in all, it appeared a pleasant place and he wondered why he had not heard more of it in the past.

He recalled the name only coming up twice before in his life. Around eight years before he had read an article in the *Times* about the war with Eastasia – or was it Eurasia, he couldn't quite recall – in which the reporter had written about the heroics of bomber pilots based at the Victory-on-Sea Aerodrome. On his way in, from the train window, he had seen that airfield, vast concrete hangars now lying empty and unused. But the lines of watchtowers and barbed wire fences were still very much in use. He'd wondered as they'd passed by a military post on the line why they still needed to guard this place so much. He'd also lamented the shutting of the base – so typical of these misguided times.

Not that he would ever say so in public of course. Thoughtcrime. Crimestop.

And the second time? Well, that had only been last month. A comrade named Murray in Sec72 had come to him and said that he'd been granted a holiday by the Party and that he was going to some place called Victory-on-Sea up north. He'd been a little jealous at the time; holidays were rare privileges. The last he had been on was a full seven years before. That had been to a place called Great Yarmouth. Much larger and scruffier than this place.

They were out of the old town now and in a newer area. The road ran parallel to the beach and all along the other side were concrete apartment buildings for tourists. Now, every couple of seconds, the bus would stop and the policeman would read a name out. Soon it was his turn.

"O'Dwyer, Brendan. Apartment number twenty-two. Report to the Party Office tomorrow morning at 09:40."

He alighted and entered the apartment. Inside it was clean, with a made-up single bed and small kitchen area. There was a bag of sugar, coffee and some powdered milk. "Doubleplusgood," he muttered to himself as much as to the telescreen playing on the opposite wall. He put a kettle of water on the hob to boil and then settled down to smoke a *Red Flag* cigarette. In the background the telescreen blared on about steel production yields being up. Usually switching off the telescreen was the first thing he did but today felt different. The constant noise was comforting almost; it helped him forget that he was alone and far from home. He watched the smoke curl into the air as the announcer switched to zinc production. Then the kettle began to whistle so he got up and made the coffee. When he sat back down again, it was talking about some act of heroism in the war against Eastasia. He lit another *Red Flag* and smoked it lazily, again muttering "Doubleplusgood." When it was finished he sipped at his tea. After that though, he could remember no more for he dozed off as a result of the exertions of the journey as the telescreen rambled on.

---

The Party office looked much like any other party office anywhere else on Airstrip one. Files everywhere, dust also, faded paint and, high on the wall, the obligatory portrait of BB emblazoned with the caption *BIG BROTHER IS WATCHING YOU* and below that, the word *INGSOC*.

The well-kept world beyond the door was kept at bay. Here, normality reigned.

"Comrade Brendan O'Dwyer reporting. I have an appointment at 09:40."

"Wait over there!"

O'Dwyer was about to remind this Outparty minion that he was Inparty Level 8 and should be spoken to properly but then stopped himself. The man would know anyway and something about his couldn't care less look bothered him. That was worrying.

Twenty minutes later he was called in. A Level 7 Inparty comrade with a strong regional accent was sitting behind the desk. He was younger than O'Dwyer, perhaps only thirty, and flabby. His appearance disgusted O'Dwyer. Twenty years ago.... Thoughtcrime. Stopcrime. The young comrade, bade him sit down and offered him a coffee. "Evans," he said, "welcome to Victory. I hope your journey wasn't too arduous."

"Doubleplusgood. The efficiency of our transportation under the watchful eyes of the Party and BB are always a wonder to me."

"Indeed. And the apartment?"

"The same. I thank BB..."

"Yes, yes, I get it. No need for all the duckspeak and newspeak here; we're a relaxed place out in the sticks. You were sent to Victory by the committee at Miniluv to get a break, a vacation, to relax, so no formalities."

"Yes, and I am thankful for it. We've had some extremely busy months down at Miniluv, curing thought criminals and the like. We must be ever vigilant! However, when they told me that I was being granted a holiday, they only gave me the outward ticket, not the return. When I questioned this, they said to speak to you."

"A return ticket, eh? No instructions from Miniluv yet but I'll let you know when I get them. In the meantime, just relax and take the break that you so obviously deserve. We have a variety performance every evening at seven in the Hall of Proletarian Toil and during the day there are bowls, tennis, badminton and a variety of other clubs. Or you can just relax by taking a stroll or having a drink, all covered by the Party of course. My personal favourite is the Chestnut Tree Café on the front."

"Chestnut Tree you say?"

"Yes. There is a large chestnut there from which it takes its name. A beautiful thing, hundreds of years old I shouldn't doubt. Plus, there's an old song, before my time but it was something like *Under the Ancient Chestnut Tree*."

"Spreading."

"Excuse me, comrade?"

"*Under the Spreading Chestnut Tree*. That was the song. Under the spreading chestnut tree, I sold you and you sold me…"

The song brought back a memory, from how many years ago? A memory of a man, one of the many, countless, nameless and almost faceless. For a reason that he had never fully understood, this one had stuck with him. He had been in love with a girl half his age, a pretty thing. He'd had her in the brightly-lit cell and yet that had not stayed with him. He…

"Yes, that may be the song. Anyway, it is a good place to relax. Also, I shall have a comrade come around for wellsex."

"It is not necessary. I…"

"The files show that your wife is dead and that your blood pressure is high."

"I thank the Party for their concern."

"Well, that is all. Enjoy your holiday here Comrade O'Dwyer."

"I will." He stood up and made to leave and then stopped and turned back. "One little thing."

"Yes, comrade?"

"The telescreen. It won't switch off."

"In Victory telescreens do not switch off."

The Chestnut Tree Café did, in fact, prove to be a pleasant place to while away an hour or more of his time. He sat down on one of the wooden chairs and a waiter bought him a bottle of *Victory* gin without him even asking. At first he turned up his nose at being presented with an Outparty drink; Inparty never drank nor smoked *Victory*, but he took it anyway and drank. There was something about this place. Inparty could always switch their telescreens off in London. Something was wrong. Thoughtcrime. Stopcrime.

Something else bothered him: why call the café the Chestnut Tree? The fact that there was a real chestnut tree next to it was one justification but it still did not satisfy O'Dwyer. The Chestnut Tree Café in London was where painters and artists gathered, as well as the old leaders of the Party, now safely unpersons. It had an aura to it that made you avoid the place. Surely the local Party knew that; BB knows everything, and so why name the café here after such an establishment even if there is a chestnut tree next to it?

He sipped at the drink, which was not as harsh as he'd expected it to be, and gazed out, trying to shake the café from his mind. The scene did not look real, like some malmemory of the time before the Revolution when he was a small child. The green grass, smart old hotels, trees surrounding the park and then, on the other side, the blue sea with the purple outlines of mountains beyond. A dream, a mirage. Thoughtcrime?

His mind went back to that other Chestnut Tree Café, somewhere near Bloomsbury. That man, Blair his name had been, Eric Blair. He had mentioned it. He had said, during those long, terrifying, intimate session in Miniluv, that he had seen Jones, Aaronson and Rutherford there years before at the very time when they had confessed to being in Eurasia. It had taken hour after hour for him to force it into Blair that if the Party said they had not been there and in Eurasia instead, then they had been in Eurasia. 'But I saw them!' he had repeated time after time, even as he had increased the voltage. But he understood in the end. They all did. Unpersons all of them. Jones, Aaronson, Rutherford, Blair. Four unpersons who had never even existed. Malmemories.

Evans was no unperson. He should have been. Back then it was unthinkable that an Inparty would be so flabby... and informal. 'No duckspeak, no newspeak; we are casual here...' Casual! How could they ever achieve victory with casual? Back then he would have been hauled to Miniluv and... what was happening to the world? To Oceania? To Ingsoc?

As he thought it, he felt ashamed. Thoughtcrime. Doubleplusungood thoughtcrime. Stopcrime!

"O'Dwyer!"

He looked up. Standing next to him was Murray from Sec72, the comrade who had told him a month ago that he had been granted a holiday here.

"I thought it was you, comrade! So, BB gave you a holiday too! Plusgood! How is Miniluv?"

"You have not been back?"

"No, still here. Waiting for my return ticket but not yet arrived."

"Ungood."

"Ungood."

---

The girl came at the hour of twenty. She was young, perhaps eighteen, and reminded O'Dwyer of his daughter Annie at that age. Except that this Outparty wellsex comrade wore no Junior Anti-Sex League sash. As the girl noiselessly removed her overalls, O'Dwyer found himself thinking of Annie. Where was she now? What was she doing? Was she real or an unperson? She had given him the greatest pride in his life when she had reported his wife for thoughtcrime.

His second wife. The first O'Dwyer himself had reported. That was what had caused his elevation to Inparty. He had worked on her himself in

Miniluv, had held her hand as he took her to Room 101. They had never been closer, never so intimate...

He exploded within the girl. She withdrew and cleaned herself. By the time he had lit a *Red Flag* and put the kettle on to boil, she was leaving. He watched her from behind and imagined that she had been Annie. That he had just had wellsex with Annie. Even though it was no thoughtcrime imagining wellsex with your daughter – there's no procreation after all – he found himself muttering "Stopcrime!" to himself between drags on the cigarette.

---

The following day O'Dwyer took a walk. He paced up and down the streets of the town, looking at the buildings, the trees, the sky and the people. O'Dwyer was used to being busy. He was always at Miniluv, always doing the Party's work. And that work was intense. It entailed staying up all night with citizens troubled by malthoughts; copious amounts of paperwork, detailing all confessions, all admissions. That was why Big Brother had recognised his need for a holiday but it was hard to switch off. He had had the same problem on his last holiday, how many years ago was that... seven... eight? It had only been for three days but he was glad to get back. Doing the Party's work was what he had been created to do, not sit around. Thinking about it all was hard.

He ended up again in the Chestnut Tree Café. Rain began to fall so he went inside and watched the rivulets trickle down the windows. They reminded him of the sweat of the unpersons whom he cured in Miniluv. They reminded him of Ingsoc, of BB.

They reminded him of Blair.

Why did he keep thinking of that case?

Not because of Blair. Blair had been unremarkable, undistinguishable from the hundreds of Outparty comrades that he'd cured over the years. Not particularly bright; wanting something but no idea what. He had been in love with another Outparty, passably pretty, but again unremarkable. Love stories were common; that was why the Party worked so hard to abolish them. Neither Blair nor Smith had taken long to break. They'd betrayed each other just as they always do.

No, he kept thinking of Blair because of himself. That was the first case he had dealt with after Annie had reported her mother. Of course, he had backed his daughter up; of course, he had seen that his wife got the treatment that she deserved. He had even offered to mete it out to her himself and for that he had been commended. Yet it had affected him. Like Blair with his Juliet Smith, he had loved his second wife. He'd tried not too; tried to make their time in bed joysex rather than crimesex, yet he had never truly mastered himself and that cut him up. He wanted to hate her yet, even as he watched her hooked up to the machine in Miniluv, he had felt pity, empathy, love. Not that he can remember the scenes now; his mind had blocked them out, but he can remember the feelings as if they were yesterday. And then along came Blair.

And it was following that case that he had his crisis. For a time, only a short time, but a time nonetheless, he began to doubt Big Brother. Looking back now, the mere thought is horrifying; he deserved to be sent to a joycamp for even having it, yet he did. He remembered lying awake at night thinking what kind of a man can do that to the woman he loves? Are we human or animal? He banished such thoughtcrime with work of course and that was that, but still… now Blair and his own doubt were inextricably linked.

And it was because of this that he wrote it.

He'd had practise writing things in oldspeak. After all, was it not him who, as part of a committee of four comrades, had composed *The Theory and Practice of Oligarchical Collectivism* by Emmanuel Goldstein, the book that had helped cure numberless unpersons? He hadn't created Goldstein of course; Goldstein had been a real person once, one of the closest comrades of Big Brother before and during the Revolution. But that Goldstein had disappeared during the first great purge. It was him however, who had resurrected him, dusted the grave dirt off his bones, and transformed him into the ultimate anti-hero, the nemesis of the Ingsoc he had helped create. O'Dwyer had enjoyed writing that book; he had found pleasure in putting himself into the mind of his evil villain, in playing with the words and putting down, in black and white, ideas that he would never normally dare breathe. It had been like a drug and, when he was finished, he had felt down and purposeless.

Therefore, it was probably no surprise that, like all addicts, he had returned to his old fix when he was down again. He would write a second book, another masterpiece and this time he would do it alone. That was a danger of course; no book in Oceania had a single author, but was still something that he could explain away if caught. Besides, he simply *had* to write it. Not for posterity; he knew that such a thing did not exist in Oceania, but for the sheer pleasure of doing it. And so, he had written the story of Eric Blair and Juliet Smith, culminating in him taking them to Room 101.

Of course, he had changed the names and lots of details. Blair became Winston Smith and Juliet, Julia. Plus, he had added elements from other unpersons he had cured and changed his name in the story to O'Brien. Plus, he'd inserted elements of his past in there too: the intellectual Syme had been a caricature of his first superior in Minitrue, a man named Hudson who spouted Ingsoc orthodoxy and was terminated in a purge, whilst Smith's recollections of his wife Katharine had been his own memories of his own wife, the first one. The only difference between them was that whereas Smith had been weak and let her leave him, when he had tired of Hilda, he had reported her to the thinkpol for excessive affection and enthusiasm during joysex and she had been terminated. He'd also placed in some deliberate errors. He wrote that Britain was called Airstrip One which, of course, was a joking moniker that it had acquired soon after the Revolution, but had never been an official title. And he pretended that newspeak was a lot more advanced than it had been at the time – it was his vision for newspeak rather than the reality. It had been – even though it was thoughtcrime to think this – a real work of art.

And then, when it was all finished, he had hidden it. He'd entered the flat of an Outparty whom he was scheduled to cure. He still remembered the name of the man: Gletkin, Arthur Gletkin. He could recall little more about him beyond the name but that had been the man. He'd found the book, started to read it and then was hauled into Miniluv. At the time

O'Dwyer had considered the move a masterstroke, since it had given him a justification for writing the book should anyone have noticed him doing so (which they surely had). He'd then hidden in another flat to repeat the process over again, but the Outparty in question had been pulled in by the thinkpol for an unbelievably careless remark at work and so was sent to a joycamp where he later became an unperson. And the book? Well, still there; a time capsule from a decade ago, undiscovered by anyone (for if it had been, he would probably be an unperson himself by now). O'Dwyer wondered if it ever would be discovered by chance one day and what people would make of it.

As he wondered, the waiter refilled his glass of *Victory* gin.

---

The next day he saw Murray again. He was walking by the beach and his old comrade from Miniluv was walking in the opposite direction. O'Dwyer was irked that he had not received any notice of his return ticket yet. He wanted to leave; he had work to do. The two men settled down and were served with gin. Then they took out the chessboard and started a game. Murray was an accomplished player and within fifteen minutes O'Dwyer was finding it difficult. By the time the clock struck thirteen, he knew he was beaten and toppled his king. They sat in silence and listened to a report on clothing production broadcast over the telescreen. Then, to O'Dwyer's amazement, Murray did something unbelievably stupid.

"I am damn well tired of all this waiting around!" the man had exclaimed. "I want to be back in London serving BB and the party but every time I go to the office, they say there is no ticket for me. It must be some bureaucratic mix-up but it really is ungood!"

O'Dwyer drank his gin and said nothing. Then they played another game where O'Dwyer lasted a full hour before toppling his king. Finally, at the hour of fifteen, he made his way to the Party office and asked to see Comrade Evans.

"Wait there!" snapped the surly Outparty at the desk.

Twenty-five minutes later he was shown in.

Comrade Murray was exactly the same as he had been before. Smug, young and flabby. 'He disgusts me!' O'Dwyer had thought to himself. 'He is everything that is wrong with today: too soft!' Then, realising the direction his thoughts were taking he stopped them. Thoughtcrime. Stopcrime.

"What can I do for you, Comrade O'Dwyer?" asked the Level 7.

"I have a crime to report."

"Go on."

"Today, in the Chestnut Tree Café, Comrade Murray expressed dissatisfaction and doubt at the workings of Ingsoc."

"In what way?"

"He was annoyed at the late arrival of his return ticket to London. He stated that it was a 'bureaucratic mix-up' and described this as 'ungood'."

"Serious charges indeed. They have been noted and justice shall be served."

"If it is of use, Comrade Evans, I can help with this. I have extensive experience curing party members of malthought. In Miniluv…"

"Comrade O'Dwyer, it is not necessary. Your devotion is noted but you are on holiday! Go back to your flat and relax. I will serve justice."

"Plusgood, comrade. I have another complaint to make as well."

"Go on."

"The Outparty on the front desk. She has been rude to me twice now, despite the fact that I am Inparty and her superior."

"Sarah, you mean?"

O'Dwyer was shocked. Referring to an underling, an Outparty by their first name! Really, standrads were slipping! "I am unaware of her name, Comrade Evans."

"Yes, she can be short. I'll have a word."

Silence reigned for a moment, as if the two men were communicating an unspoken message.

"Was there anything else, Comrade O'Dwyer?"

"My return ticket, comrade; has it arrived yet?"

"No, it has not. You may leave."

---

That night the Outparty girl came to service him again. It was as perfunctory as it had been with Hilda... or as Winston Smith had been with his Katharine. It was wellsex; sexual intercourse for health reasons only, to lower blood pressure and release pent-up fluids.

After she had left, he felt the urge to smoke but the packet in his pocket had finished so he walked over to the cupboard where the cigarettes were kept. Opening it up, he was surprised – and dismayed – to discover that the cigarettes in there were *Victory*, not *Red Flag*. *Victory* was the Outparty brand. He had smoked them on occasion in the past when borrowing one from an Outparty comrade at work and they were awful: poor quality tobacco like dust that fell out if you did not keep the cigarette level. It must be a mistake. Still, he was desperate so he opened a packet, removed one and carefully lit it. Thankfully, the tobacco stayed in and, as he sat in his armchair and reflected on the day, he found the *Victory* to be better than he'd remembered them being.

The following day, when he passed the Chestnut Tree Café, Murray was nowhere to be seen. O'Dwyer knew where he had gone; the place where there is no darkness.

And even though he had sent him there, he felt a tinge of loneliness at having no one to play chess with. He stared at the board and knocked back a gin before he realised the direction that his thoughts were taking. "Ownlife," he murmured, before then adding, "Thoughtcrime. Stopcrime."

---

But the day afterwards, at the hour of thirteen, Murray strolled into the café. O'Dwyer hid his surprise well, but inside he was confused. After Murray had downed a gin and they had begun a game, he said vaguely, "You did not come yesterday."

"Came down with an awful cold. Stayed in bed all day. Still got a bit of a sniffle now although this sea air is doing it good."

O'Dwyer said nothing. Something was wrong.

---

The days rolled by. Each the same. Chestnut Tree Café, wellsex, *Victory* gin and cigarettes. It was as if Miniluv and London were a dream. Every other day he went to the Party office and spoke with Evans. Each time the Outparty – Sarah – was rude to him and each time his ticket had not arrived. O'Dwyer did not understand it but knew better than to question.

Then, on the Friday, two weeks after his arrival, he took the risk.

"What is really happening here, Comrade Evans?" he said, sternly, firmly.

Evans smirked and he felt like punching him. "Explain your meaning, Comrade O'Dwyer."

"My ticket; why are you withholding it from me. I need it! I demand it! I am an important person in the Party, a senior figure in Miniluv. I demand my return ticket now or there will be consequences!"

"Withholding it, eh? You think I am withholding it?"

"Yes, I do. I know it."

"Comrade O'Dwyer, you know nothing! Withholding it! I am not withholding anything! Have you not realised? That return ticket is never going to arrive. It does not exist! It never will! Like your friend Murray, you are not leaving this place. The Party wants you here so here is where you shall stay."

"But why? I have work to do, thoughtcrime to root out, to punish. Goldstein's agents are as active as ever! There I can serve Big Brother; here I am just wasting time."

"Here you are serving Big Brother far more."

"I do not understand."

"No, you don't. I had wondered if you would guess by now, but no, you are either too blinkered or, more likely, too stupid."

"Comrade, I am Level 8; you are only Level 7! I..."

"Shut up O'Dwyer! Shut up you dinosaur from a useless age! Shut up you hate-ridden newspeak drone! Shut up you blinded mule of Ingsoc orthodoxy! What, the long words scare you, do they? You wish to remove them like you wish to remove anything you don't understand, cannot twist and torture into your own pathetic image!"

"Why, you Goldstein scum! I'll kill you..."

Ten minutes later they were both in the same room. Evans was not dead and neither was O'Dwyer. But the guards who had entered, restrained him, twisted his arms into some painful reverse prayer configuration, palm to palm behind his back, they had gone. Only the gag and bonds remained.

"I am sorry to have hurt you, Brendan... may I call you that? We try not to hurt, not to descend to your level these days but, alas, on occasions it is necessary." He got up from his chair, walked over to his captive and stroked his hair. Tenderly, lovingly. Like a father to recalcitrant son. O'Dwyer thought of his father; long an unperson but still shakily alive in his memory. A tear escaped his left eye.

Evans knelt down in front of him, their faces only centimetres apart, the captor's grey eyes burning into the captive's soul. He reached out and stroked that captive's cheek and then, in little more than a whisper, said, "Would you like me to remove that gag?"

O'Dwyer nodded and, carefully, lovingly, Evans unbuckled the strap and then cast it to one side. Then, in a practised and unexpected movement, he moved his face next to that of his victim and kissed him. Long and deep, mouth on mouth, O'Dwyer could feel the saliva of his assailant, the brush of his stubble, the movement of his tongue.

After several seconds Evans withdrew. "How was that?" he asked. "Did you feel anything? Did it repel you because it was deviant, sexcrime, or did you imagine that I was BB, our kiss a physical consummation of the devotion you feel for him and all that he stands for?"

"You're sick! You will suffer for this! Room 101!"

"Except that I won't. I won't suffer and I won't be going to Room 101. Not now, not ever. My superiors don't know that I enjoy embracing my patients with love but even if they did, they wouldn't care. Like I said before, you don't understand."

O'Dwyer was silent. He did not understand. He had cured countless hundreds of unpersons with malthoughts in their heads, yet never had he encountered this.

Evans stepped away. He went to a side table and came back with two glasses of gin. *Victory* gin. He put one to O'Dwyer's lips and he drank greedily.

"*Victory* gin," said Evans, smiling. "Not bad is it? Not quite up to *Red Flag* or *Revolution*, but still quite drinkable." He paused for effect and took a sip. "Now," he added. "Ten years ago it was undrinkable, but now, now it is palatable. *Victory* gin was one of the first things we changed."

"I never knew."

"No, because you wouldn't touch it. You knew what the old was like, so why would the new be any different. After all, why would we change anything? It hardly fits with the image of a boot stamping on the face of humanity for all eternity."

O'Dwyer winced at the phrase. Did they…?

"Oh yes, a nice turn of phrase. And not the only one you are capable of. In another time, another place, you could have been quite the writer."

"You knew?"

"Of course. It was retrieved four years ago."

"But you never…"

"This is a brave new world, Brendan, a new world of a new Ingsoc."

"Ingsoc does not change."

"Oh, but it does, Brendan, it does."

He settled back in his chair and took a draught of his gin. "Do you know that in Eurasia an Outparty has a flat twice the size of most Inparty members here. And they have hot water and an electricity supply that hardly ever cuts out."

"Oceania is at war with Eurasia."

"And they don't have chocolate rations – what are we down to now, a paltry fifteen grams? – but however much they want; they just pick it up off the shelves. And the women, oh, you should see the women! Like creatures from your most corrupt, most thoughtcrime dreams, lithe beauties, their uniforms clinging to their pert little bottoms and charming breasts. Not that they do much for me, of course; you know where my tastes lie, but still, for most people…"

"Oceania is at war with Eurasia."

"When I first saw it, I couldn't believe my eyes. For the first time in my miserable life – yes, that's when I realised that my life was miserable – I was jealous. I wanted something that Big Brother, that Ingsoc, could not provide. I fought it of course, but, in the end, like all of us who went there, it won out."

"Oceania is at war with Eurasia."

"Except that it is not. You know that. We haven't been at war with anyone since, when was it…? 1976. Then we realised that we all had what we needed and so agreed to stop all the senseless bombing. War is too messy, too unpredictable. Why, a bomb could land on Minitrue and disrupt our propaganda, or, even worse, Miniluv, and kill all those brave operatives like yourself, curing our enemies. Why, those enemies could even be freed, released to roam around the country and spread their Goldsteinian filth! The horror of it! So, instead, we made peace and rained false flag rockets onto our proles to keep them in check. Much cleaner and just as effective. A boot stamping on the face of humanity for all eternity. Yes, I do like that phrase, Brendan; it's as wonderful as you are."

He paused again, went over to his captive and gave him another drink of the gin. The drink was causing a warmth to flow over O'Dwyer. It was loosening his control and that bothered him.

"But there was a problem," continued Evans, taking another draught of his own gin and lighting a cigarette. "An unforeseen, unanticipated problem perhaps, but a problem nonetheless. What to do with all those materials that we would have used fighting the war? All that steel, all that coal that we mined, all those tyres. Of course, our floating fortresses and other unnecessary military hardware ate up some, but even so.

And there was something else. Since we were no longer fighting Eurasia... or Eastasia too for that matter, why not interact with them? Senior Party comrades went over there on visits and we learned from them. We became envious of them. If an Inparty in Tokyo can have six weeks of holiday a year, then why not us? If an Inparty in Warsaw can live in a house with five bedrooms and a garden, then why not us?"

"It is wrong."

"Wrong? How dare you claim such a thing? You a member of the generation that abolished right and wrong. If Big Brother says it then it is! If BB says $2 + 2 = 5$ then $2 + 2 = 5$. Well, BB says that what we did is good, doubleplusgood in fact. So there!"

"You've become soft. You've become like the old capitalists!"

"Yes, maybe we have. Do you know what, I always remembered them from the old textbooks at school? With their top hats, horse whips and ladies in wide dresses. They were meant to be figures of hate yet I always secretly envied them. I mean, who wouldn't want to live in a huge house with servants at their beck and call, fine food and drink – to a half-starved young spy then that one can be particularly appealing – and a beautiful lady at your side (alright, I admit, that bit never interested me)? Once I recall going on a spy camp. It was housed in a huge old building, Ingsoc Eternal Hall it was called, but we learned that before the Revolution it had been the residence of some particularly odious capitalist who killed coalminers and socialists. As we all denounced him in a hate session, inside I imagined the place in its splendour, with fine banquets, tables heaving with food, and those ladies in wide dresses dancing around with handsome young men under the gleam of a chandelier that actually functioned. Outwardly I hated, but inside, I loved."

"Thoughtcrime. You should be in a joycamp!"

"Maybe I should, all this oldthink and oldspeak. Which reminds me." Evans drained his gin and finished his cigarette. Then he got up and left the room. A moment later he returned carrying two large, black items. "These will suit us far better, don't you think?" He placed one top hat on the top of his own head and the second on O'Dwyer's.

"Do you know what I find so amusing?" said Evans.

O'Dwyer did not answer.

"Your manuscript. The main point where you diverged from reality was to do with newspeak. You understood the purpose of newspeak and how far it could be taken. And, if Oceania had actually developed it as much as you describe in the book, then what we, the new generation, are doing now, well, it would not even be possible. But, we got in just in time; we weren't too late. We can turn back the clock."

---

*Under the spreading chestnut tree*
*I sold you and you sold me*
*There lie they, and here lie we*
*Under the spreading chestnut tree*

*There beneath the boughs we used to meet*
*All my thoughts were so sweet*
*Eurasian hordes we'd beat-beat-beat*
*'Neath the spreading chestnut tree*

*I said "I hate you", and there ain't no if's or but's*
*He said "I love you", and the young spy shouted "Hands up!"*

The tinny music from his childhood trickled from the telescreen and the insects buzzed in the summer air. It was the lonely hour of fifteen. O'Dwyer sat at the table, a chessboard before him, his top hat on the chair at his side. Opposite was Murray. He still had his top hat on his head. Both had been sitting there for over an hour. Both had only made two moves. The waiter came round and filled their gin glasses up without asking.

The music faded and the telescreen went silent. Both men raised their heads from the game. A grave voice came over the screen: You are warned to stand-by for an important announcement at fifteen-thirty. Fifteen-thirty! This is news of the highest importance. Take care not to miss it. Fifteen-thirty!" Then the music returned.

"Must be important," commented Murray.

"Perhaps important news regarding chocolate production?" suggested O'Dwyer.

"Yes, chocolate has been concerning me. They have increased rations to fifty grams. But will we manage to fulfil them?"

"Or coffee?"

"All glory to Big Brother for promising access to coffee for all Party members, In or Out."

"BB always delivers…"

His voice drifted off and he looked out to sea. On the beach some young families played. BB had decreed that children beyond artsem were permissible, even to be encouraged, for Inparty members. And he had decreed that wellsex should exist even between spouses. His wisdom was endless!

Beyond the children were the waves, crash, crash, crashing against the shingle. In and out, ebb and flow for all eternity. Those waves had been there in his childhood, before he was born even. And they would be there after he was gone. Only BB preceded and proceeded them. Their sound magnetised and hypnotised him. It sent him racing back, as so much did these days, into his past. He thought of Blair and his Juliet; he thought of Gletkin, he thought of his mother and father and his brothers and sisters; he thought of his first wife and his second; he thought of Annie and the comrade who came to him twice a week to service him.

He thought of Murray, he thought of Evans and he thought of Big Brother...

A shrill trumpet-call pierced the air. It was the bulletin! Victory! It always meant victory when a trumpet-call preceded the news. Perhaps the chocolate quota had been met?! A sort-of electric thrill ran through the entire café. Both O'Dwyer and Murray looked up.

"Comrades! Brothers and sisters! News of the utmost importance! Big Brother in his infinite wisdom and mercy has pardoned the one-time traitor, now beloved Comrade Goldstein! Oceania is truly united; we are as one! Comrade Goldstein has been placed in charge of Miniplenty and his first decree is that from this day forward, all citizens of Oceania, be they Inparty, Outparty or proles are to be given a bicycle for transportation purposes to ease their lives and increase their productivity!"

Goldstein forgiven! Goldstein rehabilitated! Goldstein delivering greater comfort for all citizens of Oceania! What a masterstroke by BB! Who could have seen it? What genius!

The strains of *Oceania 'Tis For Thee* and the entire assembly rose. Tears flowed from his eyes as his love for Big Brother and his brave new world overtook his entire body.

***Written 23<sup>rd</sup>-25<sup>th</sup> April, 2018, Stoke-on-Trent to London, UK***

# Three Strangers

## *Juche 84*
### *(1995 CE)*

The summer heat lay heavy across the land. Insects buzzed in the breezeless air and the rich smell of vegetation wafted into every nose.

Smell though, nor warmth, can fill an empty belly.

Ok San sat on the porch of his low, white-walled and red-tiled house and surveyed the world set before him. His eyes drank in the homes of his neighbours, some living some not, some unaccounted for.

They drank in the dirt road that led to the city of Chongjin in one direction and the town of Onsong in the other.

They drank in the slopes of the hills, only two summers back thick with trees, now shorn, denuded, brown and bare.

They drank in the conical mound of the distant pit, its engines once working, now silent.

They drank in the red flags fluttering in the fields where today little grew.

And they drank in the words of wisdom carved into the hillside; words of the President, each character as high as a man.

## 세상에 부럼 없어라
### WE HAVE NOTHING TO ENVY IN THE WORLD

He closed those eyes and let the darkness take over. Then, when he reopened them, his eyes drank in something new.

Three strangers making their way along the road.

These strangers were men. They were not advanced in years and walked steadily. As they drew nearer, Ok San reckoned them all to be between forty and sixty. He also noticed that, although tanned, their skin was not that of men who spend their lives toiling in the fields. Similarly, their clothes although clean and untattered, were not ostentatious. They dressed smartly yet also simply and practically. All three wore a cap to shield them from the sun's merciless glare and pin badges denoting party membership. Most noticeably however, they looked tired and hot and hungry.

"Greetings!" he called to them.

"Good afternoon, comrade," the first replied.

"A hot day."

"Aye indeed," replied the second.

"Would you like to stop for a rest, a drink and perhaps a bite to eat? You look in need of all three."

Even as he made his offer, Ok San's stomach twisted inside. They had little enough food as it was and giving that which they did away to these strangers was madness. "Your problem is that you're too generous," his wife had chastised him on numerous occasions. "Better that way than the other," he'd always reply and it was true; how could one not offer hospitality to a hungry stranger? It was against all the rules and traditions. But then the thought of the hunger to come after he had given his own meal away passed over his mind like a shadow and he felt sick.

Ok San got up from his chair, hurried into the main room, took out the two chairs from the dining table and brought them out onto the porch, gesturing for the strangers to seat themselves. Then he went into the kitchen and poured out three glasses of water from the pail. His wife was sitting at the table weaving a basket. "Cook some rice and prepare three bowls with your best kimchi!" he commanded her.

"For who?" she asked, astounded.

"We have guests." He paused and looked her in the eyes. "Strangers passing by," he added.

"Ok San, we have little enough to feed ourselves and you want to…"

"Just do it, please."

And because his voice was firm when usually it was not and because he let her have the final word most of the time, she silently assented.

---

The three men drank their water and then wiped their brows with the dampened towels that Ok San handed them. Then, when the food was ready, they ate their meals without saying a word. But when they had all finished the first said, "That was excellent kimchi, comrade."

"My wife prepares it to an old family recipe," Ok San replied.

"Where is your wife?" asked the second.

"She is inside, weaving."

"You shall both be blessed for the hospitality you have shown us today," said the third.

From deep within the house a female laugh rang out. Ok San's wife was a marvellous woman and he loved her deeply, but she had always possessed an impudent side to her character.

The three strangers, however, were not offended. "You may not believe me now," continued the third, "but later you will do. Mark my words: before a year has passed by, you shall both be rewarded."

"Oh, we are rewarded enough," said Ok San, wishing to change the subject. "The General provides for all of our needs. Like it says on that hill over there, here in the village of Gadaenamu we have nothing to envy."

"Gadaenamu Village perhaps thinks this way, but what of Onsong Town, comrade?" asked the first stranger. "It is said that the people there are disloyal to the General and the Motherland, that they besmirch his name, cross over to China illegally, engage in capitalist activities that undermine the state and even attack officers of the police."

"We are on our way to Onsong," added the second stranger.

"But when we travel, we do so simply, without announcing ourselves," explained the third.

'What can I say?' thought Ok San. 'How can I tell them without them getting the wrong ideas?' He thought of his younger brother and his sister-in-law and their family who all lived on Toil Street in Onsong.

"It is true, comrades, that there are some in Onsong who engage in illegal activities. Everyone hereabouts knows of the markets where they sell clothes and food and other goods that they have brought across the river from China at night. And it is true too that there was a riot in the town last week in which the folk of Onsong attacked the police station in the centre of the town. But you must understand that with the shortages caused by the imperialists and the lack of rain, people are desperate. And it must be said too that the police themselves were no innocent party in all of this. They sold rice to the peasants for extortionate prices yet the bags which contained the rice said that the food had been provided free as a gift to the Korean people. This corruption makes the citizens angry and their empty bellies make them unbalanced and when people are angry and unbalanced they do stupid things."

"So you believe that Onsong should not be punished?"

"I'm not saying that exactly. Obviously, engaging in anti-state activity is a crime that is wrong, but hunger dulls minds and far from everyone in Onsong took part. Some stayed loyal."

"Like you? I sense that you still believe in the General and stay loyal to the Motherland," remarked the first stranger.

"Of course I do! How could I not? After all, I remember what the Eternal President did for us. I was born in exile; I grew up in the icy wastes of Siberia and Manchuria because my parents were forced to flee the Motherland by the tyrannical Japanese. When we finally crossed back over the Tumen to our native land tears filled my father's eyes. As a small child I remember the President and his dear wife. She was a lovely lady! She used to play with us children and teach us like a second mother. That is why I keep her picture on my wall next to that of the President." He gestured inside to the well-polished portraits.

"Yet you live here so simply," said the second stranger.

"I require nothing more. As I explained earlier, I know what exile is like."

"But if you were to ask for something from us, what would that be?" asked the third.

"I would ask for you to remember those in Onsong who stayed loyal to the General during this most arduous march."

---

# Juche 89
## (2000 CE)

The summer of the 89th Year of Juche was neither as hot nor as dry as the five that had preceded it. True, food was not as plentiful as it had been in the days of the President, and true also, that the mine on the horizon only operated intermittently and the hillsides all around the village of Godaenamu were still denuded, brown and bare. But now a new slogan adorned the slopes. Across the valley from the inspiring 'WE HAVE NOTHING TO ENVY IN THE WORLD' one could now read:

**YOUTH FOREST**

And those words have obviously had an effect for below them, in neat lines, are hundreds of saplings planted by the local young pioneers only three months before.

Ok San sits on the porch of his low white-walled and red-tiled house and his eyes drink in these youthful shoots.

They drink in too the houses of his neighbours, all occupied and accounted for now, including the building to his right, formerly empty, now the home of his brother and sister-in-law and their family.

They drink in the red flags fluttering in the fields that burst with a lush crop of rice plants.

And they drink in the dirt road that leads to the city of Chongjin in one direction and the town of Onsong in the other.

Then he closes those eyes and remembers. Everyone here remembers what happened in Onsong five summers ago although no one ever mentions it. They never mention the convoy of trucks carrying elite Korean People's Liberation Army troops from the capital, all brandishing weapons and accompanied by two rumbling tanks even though it is etched in their memories.

And they never mention either that not one of those weapons needed to be fired when the convoy arrived in Onsong's main square and the people of that rebellious town were herded onto the trucks which then took them away. Away to a Re-Education Camp. This too is etched in their memories.

They never mention too the outsiders who arrived in the town a week later and who took over the jobs and the homes of the departed. This too is etched in their memories though.

What no one ever mentions because they do not remember them are the three strangers who came to the town only a week before the army arrived. Strangers who wandered the streets and listened to the people's conversations. Strangers who searched the warehouse by the railway station that the local police chief had requisitioned. Strangers who spent hours scouring the records of the local party office.

Aside from Ok San that is. He remembers them and alone, with his wife, he mentions them. For the rest though, they remain anonymous and unknown.

But everybody does remember and talk about the list that the army officer carried with him. The list that spared a select few from the purge.

A select few that included Comrade Ok San's brother, sister-in-law and their family.

And they remember and talk too about how, out of the blue, in the autumn following that never-mentioned purge, humble Comrade Ok San was unexpectedly made Head of the Godaenamu Village Commune.

And how, the summer following that, the new Head was summoned to the capital and awarded as a Hero of Labour by none less than the General himself.

And they remember and talk freely about how well he has led their small community ever since he took over, dispensing his judgements wisely and maintaining his humility.

There is a crunch of tyres on the ground. Ok San opens his eyes and sees the black car of a party official approach in a cloud of dust. It draws up in front of his house and stops.

Three men get out of and Comrade Ok San invites them in to rest, drink and eat.

*Written 4th July, 2018, Taunton – Stoke-on-Trent, UK*
*Revised 6th July, 2018, Birmingham, UK*

# Hole in the Soul

## *2032*
## *Stoke-on-Trent*

"Sheila, I need you to check out this guy. Shinji Okamura, Male, D.O.B. 11/09/1977."

"Who's authorising this, Mark?"

"I am."

"But Mark, you know I can't…"

"Please Sheila, do it for me. I need to know as much about him as you can find."

"Mark, I…"

"Thanks Sheila, I owe you a big one."

"You sure do. I'll put it in the pile with all the others."

---

"… It is often said that a funeral is a sad occasion. However, whilst all of us here today will undoubtedly miss dad and wish he were still around, I personally do not feel sad. The fact is that Mick, my dad, lived a good life and a happy life. He did not die regretting all the opportunities that he had missed or the things he had not done. He was a man who always took life by the scruff of the neck and wrung the most out of it. He died as he lived, contented. His suffering was not long and his legacy is great. And so, Michael Pattinson, dad, may you rest in peace."

After the service was over, the number of people who came over to Mark and congratulated him on the eulogy was great. Comments like "You got him to a tee", "A real fitting tribute" and "He'd be proud of you, lad" rang in his ears. Even his son David came over and whispered, "No one could have summed up granddad better, dad." Yet it had not been hard; Mick Pattinson *had* led a happy and fulfilled life and he *had* died content. Even so, Mark still missed him. The pain of loss made his heart ache physically and the thought of never being able to sit down with his father again was too much to contemplate.

Yet that grief was also tinged with a sense of anger. Anger directed towards Shinji Okamura. Only a name on a bank statement but even so, it made his blood boil.

---

"What have you found then?"

"In short, very little. Shinji Okamura, or to be more precise, Professor Shinji Okamura, has never set a foot wrong all his life. No criminal record and no suggestion of one. Not even a speeding fine."

"Nothing? What about politics or religion?"

"An avowed, though not extreme, atheist and no political affiliations whatsoever."

"Oh, come on, there must be something. Have you checked his social media? He must have signed an online petition or posted on something in the news."

"And do you consider me to be entirely incompetent? In actual fact, two petitions signed in the last five years, one objecting to fox-hunting and the other complaining about the tardiness of the council in filling-in potholes. All posts about work or family save for a few to do with protecting dogs from abuse and the usual comedy crap. Frankly rather dull all-in-all."

"And what is his work?"

"Ahh, now that is slightly more interesting. A Cambridge academic, his specialism is in digital realisation."

"Which is what?"

"From what I can gather, doing things in digital. Like 3D models of buildings or the worlds that computer games are set in. You want to make a digital version of something and he's the guy to do it. A world leader in his field."

---

"It just doesn't make sense. A professor of digital realisation. What on earth would dad have to do with someone like that? He hated computers! I doubt he could even switch one on."

"Aw, come on, dad, that's a bit harsh! He had an iPad."

"Yeah but he didn't know how to do anything on it except Skype and that was only because I showed him. This is dodgy, the whole thing is dodgy. Why would a guy like him who was always so careful with money and wary of con-men transfer over £250,000 to some unknown professor of digital fucking realisation two years before he died."

"He had the money spare, dad."

"That's not the point. It's just so unlike him. I mean, yes, he would spend on things that he wanted, like a holiday or stamps for his collection but…"

"So maybe this Okamura had something that he wanted?"

"Or maybe he told him he did but is really a fucking con-man who swindles pensioners out of their hard-earned cash?"

"You have no proof of that."

"As if you need to tell me; I'm the cop here after all, I know all about the burden of proof. But you've got to admit, it looks dodgy."

"Sure, it does but maybe there's a perfectly logical explanation to it all?"

"Such as?"

"If I knew that I'd have told you by now."

"No, there is no other explanation. That bastard robbed my dad of quarter of a million quid and I'm not going to let him get away with it. He probably transferred it using all those digital fucking skills and dad never even realised it was gone."

"Now you're talking bollocks, dad. Granddad was of pretty sound mind right up until he died. He'd have noticed. He was always on the ball with money."

"So, what do I do, David, what do I do?"

"You know what I'd do?"

"What's that?"

"Ask Doug Fellows. He was granddad's best mate and he knew him longer than any of us. Talk to him. Perhaps he let slip some clue or hint to Doug."

"That's a good idea. Damn good. Wish I'd thought of it."

"You should have. You're the cop after all. Say, how much do you get paid for solving a mystery?"

"What's that meant to mean?"

"Well, I could do with a bit of extra cash. Uni life isn't cheap you know; not like your day when it was all free."

"I gave you a good sum last time you were home. Get a job!"

"I have, in a pub, five nights a week. But a little extra wouldn't go amiss..."

"Nice try, son, nice try!"

---

Doug Fellows' living room reminded Mark of his father's. It was full of junk – some valuable, most not – accumulated during a well-lived life. There were several clocks, some toby jugs, diecast models of vintage cars, a world map in gold that looked as if it might have come from a Readers' Digest offer and a framed and signed photograph of Sir Garfield Sobers.

"Won that at Edgbaston in '95," said Doug when he saw Mark looking at it. "Your dad was with me that day. We went to two tests together every year for the past half a century, give or take. Great cricketer was Sobers, an absolute legend."

"Indeed. Though that whole West Indies team was pretty formidable."

"Never been anything like them and probably never will be. It's such a shame that the West Indies seem to have given up on test these days. Damn fine one-day side of course, but it's not the same."

Such comments reminded Mark as to why his dad and Doug had been such good friends. The test versus one-day thing had come up almost every time he had spoken with his father. Conversations that were now no more.

"But you're not here to talk about cricket, are you? So, what can I do for you, Mark?"

Mark sat down and took a sip of the tea that Doug had made him. "It's about dad," he began, "and something curious. Does the name Professor Shinji Okamura mean anything to you?"

"Cambridge professor?"

"That's the one."

"Oh yes, I know the name. your dad went to see him on a number of occasions a few years back. I went with him twice although I never met Okamura himself. I tagged along for the ride as it were. Went around the Fitzwilliam whilst they had their meeting. Afterwards we met up again and attended Evensong at St. George's Chapel. Your dad wasn't a religious man of course, neither am I particularly for that matter, but that building is exquisite; the finest piece of Anglican architecture in the world in your dad's opinion."

"What was their meeting about?"

"Truth be told, I don't know. He never told me and I never asked. They had some business together; it was professional, not personal. I do recall your dad saying that they were both involved in some project. Must have been big though since he went down quite a few times, about ten in all I reckon, although I only accompanied him twice, and the meetings were several hours long both the times I was there."

"Did he seem intimidated or uneasy on those occasions?"

"No, not at all. In fact, he came out rather happy if anything. The second time we stopped over and had drinks in the Eagle. It was a cracking night! But why do you ask?"

"Two years before dad died he transferred a quarter of a million quid out of his account into that of this Shinji Okamura. It was a large chunk of his savings. I reckon he might have been duped by a con-man."

"And I doubt that is the case since he seemed pretty on-the-ball each time we went there. However, I will admit, it *is* rather strange and it certainly *is* a lot of money. But I don't have the answer to your mystery although I know who will have."

"And who's that?"

"Professor Okamura of course? Why don't you ring him up and ask?"

The A14 had been busy. As always crammed with lorries making the trip to and fro Felixstowe, an endless train of containers bound for every part of the British Isles. 56mph max if you're lucky.

Consequently, when Mark arrived at the Cambridge Science Park office block where Professor Okamura had agreed to meet him, he was tired, irritable and in no mood for anything.

Okamura looked like Mark expected he would. Short, black-haired and impassive. The stereotype of an Oriental academic. When he opened his mouth though, there was a surprise. No clipped sounds here, instead a rich Edinburgh burr. "Nay what you expected, eh?" said the professor upon seeing his visitor's surprised expression. "My dad came to the UK to work when I was aged six. I've stayed ever since. I'm more British than Japanese these days. Come this way."

He showed Mark to a large, airy office and then offered him a cup of tea. After that, he sat down and said, "I suppose you've come about the quarter of a million quid."

"I suppose I have. It was a shock. Dad never mentioned anything about making an investment like that and in the bank records it says that he transferred the money directly to your personal account."

"It wasn't an investment, Mr. Pattinson and, yes, he did transfer the money directly to me. You see, what we did was professional but not through the university or any third party."

"And what did you do?"

"What I did was put an advert out four years ago in a national newspaper asking if anyone was interested in taking part in a research project on memory which I was leading. A number of people applied, several of them were selected and your father was one of them. He undertook the project and we became acquainted. At the end he was so impressed with the results that, a year or so later, he contacted me privately. He wanted to take it further and was willing to pay me to do so. I agreed and so we did. That was what the money was for."

"A research project on memory! Do you really expect me to believe that? My father was not a medical man, he had no interest in such things!"

"Whether you choose to believe me or not is entirely your prerogative, Mr. Pattinson. However, it is the truth."

"So, what was this research project then?"

"It is hard for me to describe, but much easier to demonstrate."

"Demonstrate?"

"Yes, show you the results. I am allowed to do that and so am happy to oblige."

Mark was intrigued. He was still suspicious but this guy did sound genuine and not like your average con-man. But then the best of them do come across that way. "Go on then," he said.

"Come this way, please."

Professor Okamura took him down a corridor to a room. It looked like any small meeting room in any company save for the fact that it had an impressive-looking computer in one corner with a load of wires and devices attached to it. In the middle was an armchair. "Sit there, please," said Okamura.

Mark sat.

"Now Mr. Pattinson, please tell me, what is your most precious memory of your father?"

"Why on earth do you need to know that?"

"Bear with me, please. The logic in what I am asking will become apparent very soon. This is important: which shared memory with your father is the most precious?"

Something in the professor's voice and expression told him that this was worth doing. "I don't know, there are so many to choose from. He was a great dad. Family holidays, the football, just chats together…"

"I need something more specific, Mr. Pattinson."

"There was a campsite. In Wales. We used to go there every year, me and him. It was a beautiful place, in a river valley with mountains on either side. Very basic but really beautiful. We'd make a campfire, put our beers to cool in the river and just sit there, chatting and looking at the flames."

"Very good. Right, now I need you to put this helmet on."

The 'helmet' was more like a metal ball with wires protruding from it. There was no visor or way to see out of it. With some trepidation, Mark put it on. His entire world went pitch black. He was about to remove it when there was a faint hiss of gas and he passed out.

---

*He was at the campsite. The river was to his left and the tent to his right. High above them the mountains rose, thick with pine trees. The sky was cloudy as it always is in Wales and there was a faint smell of sheep and fresh vegetation on the air but the strongest odour was that of the campfire. The waters of the river gurgled merrily. In front of him was a camping chair, the orange one that dad had bought when he was about ten and getting too big for the child's chair that he'd had before.*

*And sitting in the camping chair was him.*

*It was a younger Mark Pattinson, perhaps only twelve years old. He was talking excitedly about the project they'd been doing at school and what his mate Ashton had said to the teacher. Ashton. Ashton Walker. Why, he hadn't seen him for twenty years or more! Insects buzzed around*

*them and a bird called. He was there, back in the campsite with his dad.*
*Not just similar but actually there!*

*He had travelled back in time.*

*Except that now he was his dad watching him. It was weird but magical.*

*He had travelled back in time.*

---

"How long was I out?"

"About an hour."

"I travelled back in time!"

"No, you did not."

"But it seemed so real. It was real! I can remember it now, vividly, as real as any memory."

"That, Mark, is the whole point."

---

"It is called Memory Reconstruction. The computer scans the client's brain and uploads all their memories. However, as you are doubtless aware, memories deteriorate quickly over time. Think back to your childhood and you only get snippets, glimpses, faded and unclear. Often faces, even those of the people closest to you, are lost or so degraded as to become unrecognisable. Can you picture your father's face, Mr. Pattinson?"

"Yes, but you're right, it's unclear and he only died a few weeks ago."

"Indeed. Other factors can also distort your perceptions. The face of your father that you see; is it from an actual memory or instead a photograph that you have viewed more recently? Photographs can fossilise faces until all we recall is that which is on the image before us."

"That is a good point."

"With the latest brain mapping techniques however, we can now scan memories and download them. That has been possible for some time and will be of great interest to the historian or the detective like yourself in the future. But that is not my domain. Instead, I work more like a photo restorer. I take the memories that are most important and restore them to their full glory. And, interestingly, the memory most precious to your father was also the one that you cited: the campsite. Those times were extremely special to him; I know because he spoke about them at length. That is why we chose that memory to restore."

"But how? You can't go back in time and recapture it."

"No, that is true. But I can go to the location, take videos and do 3D modelling. Capture sounds and smells. Then, by combining this with the degraded original, a HD memory is created."

"So, it's not so much a restoration as part real, part new creation."

"Yes, but then you'll find that to be the case with most restorations in the world, be they buildings, photos, cars, paintings or whatever."

"And then you implant that in the brain?"

"Precisely, using that helmet that you have just worn. Your father's memory is now your memory. Your brain can return to it and view it again and again. Of course, it will degrade as all memories do, but the difference is that this memory is now on disk so, when it degrades too much, you can implant it again, thus it always retains its freshness."

"Incredible!"

"I know. It is an unbelievable thing. Your father just signed up for the initial project for the free travel and accommodation in Cambridge, but once he had tasted what we can do, then he was transfixed."

"So, he paid you the money for this camping memory?"

"No, that was part of the original project. Each participant was allowed to choose five separate memories on a disk. That was one of the ones he chose. They were also offered a helmet to buy. He purchased one."

"So, the quarter of a million was for the helmet?"

"No, they are only ten thousand and that was paid to the university. The larger fee was for something else, something that he asked for."

"Which was?"

"That, I am afraid, I cannot reveal. He gave me strict instructions never to reveal the details of our project to anyone, even his family, even after his death. I am honour-bound to respect those wishes, hard though that may be for you. However, unless he has destroyed it, the disk will still be at his house along with the helmet, but it is password-protected and I cannot reveal that password as he never told it to me. I am sorry I cannot be of more use to you."

"But can't you tell me anything more? I mean, if this was important to him, I need to know! Which memories were they? Did they involve me?"

"No, Mr. Pattinson, they did not involve you. Nor too did the majority of this project involve memories in the strictest sense. This was not a restoration project; it was pioneering, taking things to the next frontier. I can say no more save that there was a hole in your father's soul and I am happy that I helped to fill it."

---

He found the helmet easily enough. It was at the back of the wardrobe in his father's bedroom. Easily accessible. He probably used it a lot. He did not even need to look for the disk; it was already inserted. But, as the professor had asserted, it was password protected. None of the usual passwords worked and so Mark took it to the local computer specialist. He couldn't help so Mark went to a hacker who had done some unofficial work for the police on occasions. The hacker was intrigued by the helmet but could not crack the disk. The security was far more advanced than usual. So, it seemed that Michael Pattinson's secret had gone with him to the grave.

---

Mark did not hear the doorbell because he was mowing the lawn and the racket of his dad's old Flymo drowned out everything else. He did, however, see Doug Fellows when he walked around the back and waved at him. He switched the mower off and came to greet his old friend.

"I'm driving down for the Edgbaston Test tomorrow and I thought I'd pop in and see how you are bearing up. I don't blame you for moving into your dad's old house, it's a lovely place and so nice to see it being used."

They drank tea together on the terrace and talked test. Then, as it inevitably would, the conversation turned towards the late Michael Pattinson. "Did you ever get in touch with that professor in Cambridge?" Doug enquired. Mark told him the whole story and then showed him the helmet and disk. The retired IT specialist was fascinated, asking about how it worked and what the experience of the camping trip memory had been like. "It's strange," Mark told him, "but I can still remember it now, as if it were my own memory, except that I'm looking at things through dad's eyes."

"Hmm, and tell me again, what did this Okamura say about your dad's special project."

"Nothing much, that's the problem. Only that it was not a memory restoration per se, but instead something more. 'The next frontier' was the phrase he used. That and the enigmatic, 'you father had a hole in his soul'."

"A hole in his soul... hmm... I wonder... Put that thing on me will you, yes... that's it, I see, now, how do we enter the password...? Excellent. Let's try this... no, didn't work... with a capital letter... aha! Mick, you old romantic, I can read your bloody mind! Mark, I'm in!"

*I am walking down the road in a city. A city that is familiar to me, Leeds maybe, no, Sheffield. But the Sheffield of half a century ago with Austins and Hillmans on the roads. It is raining. There is a bus stop. I have a bus to catch. I decide to run for the shelter to get out of the rain. I arrive in it. There is another passenger waiting. My God, she's beautiful! Long dark hair and brown eyes. I smile at her and she smiles back. "My name's Mick," I start to say…*

*… and we're walking down the lane, a beautiful country lane. She has her arm around me and her head on my shoulder. It is a beautiful summer's day. We come to a stile and climb over it, me helping her. She wears a floral-patterned dress and the breeze whips her hair across her face. I brush it clear and kiss her on the lips. She squeezes my hand. We lie in the meadow and watched the fluffy clouds scuttle past, still holding hands, our lives completely in sync…*

*…the setting sun drops slowly behind the massed temples. Gongs are sounded and a horn is blown. We sit in silence gazing out at the massed worshippers, thousands of brown bodies, old and young, rich and poor, humanity momentarily as one in communion with the divine. Neither speaks nor wishes to. There is no need. We understand one another, our hearts as one. A baby cries out as its mother pours Ganges water over its head. In the distance a flaming corpse drifts past on its bier. The entire cycle of humanity like a wheel and we are at the centre…*

*…she puts down her fork and knife and smiles at me. She stands up and takes my hand. We climb the narrow staircase of our home, our beautiful cottage that we have bought, furnished and cared for together. As we reach the landing I gaze out of the small window at the snow-covered, pine-clad valley beyond. I feel the warmth of the log fire that she lit earlier in the bedroom. We are in the bedroom. I divest myself of my clothes and she pulls off the jeans that do such justice to her perfect figure. Our mouths meet and we collapse onto the bed. I enter her with uncontrolled passion and heaven's gates open for us both.*

"Her name was Eve Hitchens and she was a girl that he dated at university. I remember it well. He came into the house one evening telling us all about the 'cool chick' that he'd met at the bus stop. First love and all that I suppose, but he thought the world of her. They went out for a few months but I guess that she wasn't as into him as he was her. She dumped him for another guy just before Christmas and he was heartbroken."

Doug had spent over an hour in the helmet and had come out of the experience with a look of unrestrained joy upon his face. Mark had asked him what had happened but he just put the helmet on his old friend's son and started the programme again. When he came out, Mark asked one simple question: Who was she?

"But that doesn't tally, Doug; you say that the relationship lasted only a few months yet what I experienced in there – and can remember as clear as day now – was something much longer and more serious. She grew older, they travelled the world, they lived together and there was no other guy. Do you know what this means? Dad must have been having an affair for years that he never told anyone about, even after he was with mum. No wonder he wanted Professor Okamura to keep it all so quiet. The old rogue! Do you know what, that has kind of dimmed my view of him a bit; I mean, it's not exactly very moral is it?"

"It would not be if that were the case, but it was not. Mark, you are forgetting what the professor told you. His project with your dad was not about the restoration of memories, it was the next frontier, fixing a hole in the soul."

"I don't get you."

"Your dad never did have an affair, he was faithful to your mum and Eve Hitchens did dump him only a few months after they got together. I know that, I was there; it nearly destroyed him. He was laid low for months, awful to watch and even years later, after he got together with your mum and even after they split up, he still held a candle for his first love. He never contacted her but he often wondered what she was up to. Only a few years ago, after a lengthy session in the pub, he talked to me about her, about how he had enjoyed a good life, fulfilled all his goals and was entirely content and happy save for one thing: What if?"

"What if?"

"What if they had stayed together. What if it had worked and he and Eve had joined their lives; would it have worked? Would he have achieved greater happiness or less? Was she the one that he had been destined to be with? He was an old romantic after all."

"But the memories on the disk!"

"Are not real. Okamura told you, they are not restorations of original memories, well, aside from the meeting at the bus stop. They are new creations, an attempt to explore what it would have been like had his life taken a different course. He had always wanted to explore India with her; in these false memories he does. He had always dreamed of living in a little cottage in Snowdonia with her; in these false memories he does. Yet he had never dreamed of a harsh separation, her dying before him, infidelity and all the other hateful things that reality throws at us. Did you not notice that there was none of that there, not a single argument, crossed word, nothing. It was all perfect, some dreamy romance like in that Swedish film Elvira Madigan that your father loved where they lark about in summer meadows, hold hands at sunset and everything is perfect and eternal. All except for that fact that in that film they commit suicide at the end; your father's version is better, it just drifts away into the clouds."

"It all seemed so real."

"Because they are memories, just like any memories, implanted into the brain in the same way. The only difference is that these ones are artificially-created. That is the next frontier you see: Okamura has rewritten history."

---

This time, instead of sunshine, there was rain pounding at the window of Professor Shinji Okamura's office.

And this time, instead of just one man sitting on the opposite side of the desk, there were two.

"So, I take it from your phone call and the fact that you are sitting here, you have managed to guess the password and experience the disk."

"That is correct."

"So, now you know. What more is there for me to say?"

"A hell of a lot," began Doug Fellows. "What you have done, it is... it is diabolical! You should be imprisoned!"

Okamura sat back in his chair. "And you, Mr. Pattinson, do you share your father's friend's opinion?"

"Yes and no. We have talked about this at great length, my son too. He takes the opposite view to Doug; he things it's wonderful, a miracle. I am unsure. I can see both sides."

"Please elaborate."

"Well, on the one hand what you have achieved is, technologically-speaking, unbelievable. And it can bring great happiness to people: those who have suffered bereavement and wish to remember their loved ones in a better – and happier – fashion, the homeless and drug-addicted, victims of child abuse and other such horrors. The hell that they have endured is unimaginable and is often what is stopping them from moving forward with their lives. Give them a clean sheet, a happy childhood, a past free of abuse and torture and the gains can be immeasurable. But then, conversely, what you are doing is trying to rewrite history. What if the government or the military starts planting false memories in our minds, or the mafia. Your technique could wean people off drugs but it could also lure them towards the. Even my father's seemingly harmless example can have its drawbacks. It cured the hole in his soul, but what of Eve Hitchens, what would she think of all of this if she knew. Would it amuse her or appal her? Isn't it the grossest possible breach of privacy, rewriting someone's life story? I am torn I suppose."

"Then our views tally, Mr. Pattinson. When your father first approached me with the idea, I rejected it. But I am a scientist and scientific curiosity is impossible to control. It meant a lot to him and, besides, if I refused him, then who is to say that the next guy won't? Because of wat we have achieved already, this was always going to be attempted and, since the jump is, scientifically-speaking, not a large one, the attempt would be successful. After all, we can already implant memories and design new ones to patch up the old. The leap is not a giant one."

"Scientifically perhaps, but morally it is enormous!" protested Doug. "You are playing God!"

"As is the sheep breeder or the designer of drugs that cure cancer and lower blood pressure. Where does man's work end and God's begin? No one can answer that. The lines are unclear."

"It is wrong!"

"And perhaps you are right. I developed this, I tested this and I have succeeded with this. However, I have not marketed it nor made any money out of it, for that which your father paid merely covered the costs. I haven't even patented it yet. Should I? Should the cat be let out of the bag or not? I can keep it quiet but who says that the next man will not? Answer me those questions please, because I cannot."

There was silence. Neither could Douglas Fellows. Neither could Mark Pattinson.

Outside the rain hurled itself against the window panes and the sky was grey.

"More tea?" asked Shinji Okamura.

---

David bids goodbye to his dad, ends the call and puts his phone in his pocket. So, the meeting with the Japanese professor had delivered some unexpected results. He can't wait to hear more about it... and to try out that helmet again. He glances at his watch. Forty minutes until his shift starts. He could walk it but in this rain...

At the stop the digital display says that the next bus is due in ten minutes. He sits down. There's only other passenger: a girl his age. Long dark hair and large brown eyes. 'My God!' he thinks, 'she's beautiful!' He smiles at her.

She smiles back.

*Written Birmingham New Street – Lincoln, Lincoln – Stoke-on-Trent, Stoke-on-Trent to Liverpool Central & Moorfields to Stoke-on-Trent, 16th-19th July, 2018*

# Unto China

*'Pull a thread here and you'll find it's attached to the rest of the world.'*
**Nadeem Aslam**

## Part 1

*Nottingham, UK*
*2018*

Click!

It started with a camera.

Click! Click!

How stupid is that?

Click! Click! Click!

But that is the truth.

Rashida sneaked the camera in that her cousin Amin gave her when she went home. It was a pretty poor thing, one of those that printed off the pictures immediately; photos that came out blurred and indistinct. But even so, there in the lights-out, hushed-whispers secrecy of the dormitory, the air thick with things forbidden, it was as magical as the genie's lamp in Aladdin. Pictures were forbidden, everybody knew that; pictures were a way of trying to copy creation, to become a God oneself, the ultimate sin. And photography was even worse, for did not people smile, pose and try to look beautiful when in a photo? Immodest. Bringing attention to the self. Narcissistic. Fitna. An entire litany of sin.

But they treasured those blurred images, schoolfriends laughing together, time itself captured, and then hid them in places unknown. Spies though, exist everywhere and less than a week later the headmistress herself came to the dormitory and searched. She knew where to look. All those in the photographs were severely reprimanded. Rashida was never seen again in the Jamia al-Hudaa Residential College for Girls.

Click!

Gone in an instant.

The next month I went home, from the pious protection of the school's four walls to the similarly sanctified and safe confines of my father's house. Yet something had changed; that camera had unleashed a genie that would not get back into its lamp. I remember as vividly as if it were yesterday gazing out of the window of the car as we drove through the busy city streets. I saw a group of gorah girls with their heads and faces uncovered, laughing and happy. How could they be like that whilst so immersed in sin? How could Allah allow it. I looked at my mother beside me, the very picture of piety. Why didn't she ever smile like that?

Why didn't I?

That was it. That was when I realised. Somehow, deep down, it clicked that I had not been given the entire truth.

Click!

That holiday I started going out. I told my mum and dad that I was visiting Sameera or Zaeba but it wasn't true. Instead I took the bus into town and wandered around the streets. I looked at the people sitting in the coffee shops or browsing in the shops. And they looked at me too; harsh looks as if to say, 'And what are you doing here, Paki?' At first, I feared them but after a couple of days I no longer noticed.

But after three days I noticed something new. It was a large building next to the market. On the front it said Library. 'Islam instructs us to seek knowledge even unto China,' the teachers continually taught us at school. Well, I could not go to China, I was not even allowed in Huddersfield, but of the places set before me, where better to seek knowledge than a library. I went inside.

Behind the desk sat a woman. That reassured me immediately. I would not have felt comfortable speaking with a man, but a woman was different. This one had a nice smile but even so, I was a little wary of her. She was black, a black as coal and her teeth gleamed like pearls in her face. I reminded myself that the Prophet himself (peace be upon him) had chosen a black as the first to sound the Call to Prayer. Bilal. I went up to this female Bilal and shyly asked, 'Excuse me, can anyone use the library?'

That question changed my life.

Of course, I was told that anyone could and, more than that, she even explained it all to me and signed me up as a member. More than that though, she befriended me. Maybe it was the novelty of a Muslim girl who had never set foot in a library before, or maybe she was just the friendly type, but this strange black woman who introduced herself as Grace, took me under her wing and guided me. 'So, what books are you looking for, Someya?' she asked.

'I don't know precisely. Perhaps books about freedom? I am interested in freedom.'

'Freedom? My sister, there is nothing greater to be interested in! You want freedom, then I shall find it for you. Here, take this one, it is excellent. You will love it I am sure.'

The book was called The Long Walk to Freedom and it was about a man named Nelson Mandela. 'He is the greatest exponent of freedom in the world,' she told me. 'He makes me proud to be a South African. For twenty-seven years they locked him up, beat him, belittled him. But at the end of it all he refused to hate and instead embraced his old captors. What a man! Read this book!'

So, I did and each page inspired and captivated me. I hid it under my pillow and when mum asked I lied and told her that it was a collection of hadith. Two days later I returned to the library and gave the book back to the black woman. 'Did you enjoy it?' she asked.

'It was amazing,' I replied. 'Do you have anything else like it?'

'As it happens, I do. I was thinking about your request and I guessed that I would see you again and so I picked out this one. It's another story of freedom but this time the hero is an Indian like you. However, I have always had a special connection with this story too because this Indian, Gandhi, also had his awakening in my home country. Indeed, it was near to my hometown itself, a place called Pietermaritzburg. He was thrown off the train there for not being white. Many times have I waited for trains myself on that very station and thought, if it were not for that Indian man then maybe I too would not have been allowed to travel. It is amazing how the life of one can impact onto another even if we do not realise it.'

This second book affected me more than the first. Maybe it was because I was more familiar with the culture of this Gandhi, I do not know, but his story really hit home. He was so simple and pure, always refusing to use violence and ready to protect those even not of his own kind. Yes, he inspired me but he also confused me. All my life I had been taught that there are Muslims and then there are the People of the Book and then, beyond them, there are the idol worshippers who are the most misguided of all. Yet this man was one of them, one of the most religious of them and very educated too, and his faith inspired him to great things. Set beside him, both the Congress politicians and the Muslim League seemed the corrupt and misguided ones.

He made me angry too. Angry that in school they had never mentioned either him or Nelson Mandela.

Following Gandhi, I read about many others, men and women who had changed the world for the better by the strength of their will and beliefs. Nonbelievers and believers who did not see the world through narrow glasses and who did not discriminate by creed, skin, sin or anything else.

Thanks to them – and Grace, my guide through the forest – my life was changed irrevocably.

I went back to school and tried to be the same submissive Someya as I had been before. But now the words of the teachers who more like clashing gongs or clanging symbols and the limits of their knowledge abundantly clear. I endured them for a term, but beyond that I could suffer no more.

Which is why I am now sitting on a train heading for Shanklin, a place that has significance for me. It is the place where I first entered bondage five years ago and it is the place where I shall set myself free.

After all, like it says in the book that I have here on my lap.

I have nothing to lose but my chains.

# Part 2

*Pietermaritzburg, South Africa*
*2003*

The heat that day had been sweltering. Thirty-five degrees maybe; well in excess of the usual. Sweat had poured from her brow all day long and her back felt sodden. It was cooling now as the sun sank slowly from its zenith in the sky, but lethargy and warmth still engulfed her entire being. She needed a drink.

Miriam Mzamane sat down on the bench provided by the Passenger Rail Agency of South Africa with a long sigh. She did not notice the glory of the colonial-era red-brick station buildings, nor the plaque marking the spot where the Mahatma Gandhi had been thrown off a train due to his ethnicity back in 1893. Instead, all she noticed were the pains from the blisters in her feet and the joints in her fingers where the heavy bags that she was carrying had dug in without mercy. She sighed again. What she would do for a shot of mampoer! Only two or three years ago she could complete such a walk and carry such weight without a problem and yet now... ach! Age, it comes to us all!

As her breathing recovered and her heart began to slow down its beats, she glanced up at the clock. A quarter past four. A full three hours until the little train to Ixopo would be chugging its way out of the station to take her home. Three hours on the platform alone and with nothing to do and almost five hours before she could get a drink. She rummaged in the string bag by her right leg, brushed her hand against the empty flask and then fished out a small satsuma. Carefully, she peeled it, putting the peel in a neat pile by her side before popping the first segment into her mouth.

The sweet juices ran over her tongue and down her throat. She closed her eyes and savoured the taste. Mmm... These had looked to be good fruit when she had seen them on the stall and she was not mistaken. Yes indeed, sweet and refreshing...

'Excuse me Nkosazana, do you mind if I sit there?'

Opening her eyes, she saw her vision filled by the outline of another lady. She was large and she wore a broad grin of pearl white teeth. Something about her was vaguely familiar but Miriam could not work out what. 'Of course, Nkosazana, sit there; the seat is free.'

'Thank you.'

Yes indeed, this lady was indeed familiar somehow, but from where? 'Your accent Nkosazana, I think that it is from Ixopo; am I mistaken or not?'

'No, you are precisely right. That is my town. In fact, I am just returning from visiting that place, but now I am waiting for the Shosholoza Meyl service to Johannesburg.'

'And I am going the other way, back home to Ixopo. I thought you looked familiar somehow yet I could not place you. I must know you from home. Pray tell me Nkosazana, what is your name and family?'

'Grace Makwetu at your service.'

'Makwetu, Makwetu... hmmm, that is a Xhosa name, indeed my husband had family of that name, but I do not recall you.'

'Your husband is late, Nkosazana?'

'Maybe so, maybe not. We are separated you see. Perhaps he is late, perhaps still alive. He went to the city five years ago and that was the last that I heard of him. The city swallows people up and we never hear of them again.'

'Nkosazana, that is so true.'

'Please, Grace, no more formalities. My name is Miriam, Miriam Mzamane.'

'There are Mzamane on Margaret Road I think.'

'Yes, they are my people.'

'Nkosazana, the world is a small place, is it not? We think that it is huge but when it is all boiled down, we are just tribes, all connected.'

Miriam nodded in agreement, but behind her smile and lack of words, her mind was on fire. Who was this woman? A Makwetu, the same tribe as her husband, Desmond, and yet she did not know her. How could this be? She had met all the Makwetu countless times. Yet the woman was unlikely to be a liar; she had the Makwetu look about her; indeed, she seemed vaguely familiar, and she certainly knew the peoples of Ixopo. The mystery gnawed inside her. To cover her tracks, she offered a satsuma to the stranger.

'Why, thank you, Nkosazana,' said Grace, taking the fruit.

Miriam decided to take the plunge. 'Say, do you know of a Desmond Makwetu?' she asked.

Quickly, perhaps a little too quickly, Grace shook her head. 'Desmond, no, I do not know him. I am a Makwetu, it is true, but my people are many and I am not good with names. Maybe I have met him but I do not recall the name. Is he a friend of yours?'

'He was my husband... or is.'

'The city?'

'The city.'

The two women munched on the sweet juicy fruit and gazed at the mountains beyond the railway tracks.

'What caused him to go there?'

Perhaps because this was a stranger, or perhaps because no one had asked her that question even at the time when it happened, Miriam decided to answer honestly. 'I am not so sure. Our marriage was not so bad. We did not have children which is always hard, but we laughed together and did not accumulate debt. But even so, there was something in his heart that was not right. Some place that I could not visit. At times I would come across him and he was crying like a woman with no explanation. I tried to comfort him, but it did no good. I tried to be a good wife.'

'I am sure you were.'

'But he still left. One day he was there and the next he was gone. He went on a business trip of two days to the city. But when he did not appear on the Friday evening I was worried. All weekend I was on edge, fearful that he had been robbed and killed. Then, a week later I received a letter. It included some money and four words: Sorry. I love you. That was five years ago.'

'Your burden is heavy, Nkosazana.'

'It was, but I grew used to it. I still worry for him, there in that place, with all those terrible people. The city eats good people whilst the evil thrive. I pray for him.'

'Do not fear; he is alright. Of that I am sure.'

The silence took over again. Miriam offered Grace another satsuma. A freight train clanked past, the smell of oil reaching their nostrils, forty waggons all headed north.

'And so Nkosazana, you know my tale. What about yours?'

'Mine is the mirror of your own I suppose. Unlike you, I was the one who left my marriage and went to the city. My spouse was a good person, but they did not understand me. No one did, not in Ixopo. So, I had to leave and go elsewhere. Like your husband, I went to the city where I could be myself. There is great evil in that place, that much is true, but there is also hope and freedom if you know where to look. That is why I only came back to Ixopo to visit. That is my past, not my present; I have moved on.'

The last waggon rolled past their eyes and then it was gone, only the smell remained and a faint clatter as it traversed the points north of the station. In Miriam's eyes, that train was like life; here now, gone tomorrow. Whether we are better or worse for it is hard to say.

'You have well-laden bags,' Grace said. 'What are you cooking tonight?'

'Oh, tonight I cook samp, my mother's own recipe with both beef and lamb. I boil the meat on the bone for an hour first; it really brings out the flavour and I also add a small amount – two teaspoons maximum – of curry powder. It gives it something special.'

'I can taste it already. It sounds wonderful.'

'It is Desmond's favourite dish. He is always so happy when I cook it.'

She realised that she was now talking about him in the present tense and silently admonished herself for it. How can a man gone for five years be anything but late? And why should she feel any affection for a man who left her in the lurch without so much as a goodbye? No, he deserves no such affection.

Yet even as she thought those thoughts, she remembered him crying all alone in their bedroom; tears expressing a deep unhappiness that she never understood despite years of asking him, trying to comprehend, putting his head on her shoulder. Without realising, a tear trickled from her left eye.

Miriam was broken from her reverie by a delicate touch. A handkerchief wiped that tear away. Holding it was Grace Makwetu, a stranger and yet of the same tribe as the man whom she had been crying about. 'Thank you,' she whispered. Grace said nothing but put her arm around her and stared at the sun.

And there they stayed, for minute after minute, as the mountains changed from green to gold and the sky was slowly dyed a rich salmon pink.

The Shosholoza Meyl service to Johannesburg rolled into the station and stopped before them. Grace Makwetu stood up and faced the stranger that she had befriended. 'Nkosazana, I must leave now, but I am glad that I have met with you today. Please, do not cry and do not fear for Desmond. He is safe and well; he prospers in a place where he can be who he truly was, intlunkulu encinane.'

And with those words she left, climbing onto the carriage as the wheels slowly ground their way out of the station.

Miriam sat there in stunned silence. Then she stood up and walked across to the small plaque that marked the fact that Gandhi was thrown off a train here a hundred years before. She knew the words off by heart, so many times had she read them. 'This incident changed the course of his life'.

And that day, at the same place, her own life was also changed. Intlunkulu encinane – my little sparrow. Only one person had ever called her that; only one person had ever loved her that much. Now she knew why her husband had been so unhappy, why he had left her and why he would never come back.

And why Grace Makwetu had looked so strangely familiar.

# Part 3

*Pietermaritzburg, British Bechuanaland*
*1893*

'Rules are the basis upon which all civilisation is built. You may not like them, may not always be able to see the purpose in them. But they exist to protect us. Abandon the rules and you open the doors to chaos.'

Those were my grandfather's words. I remember them well. His crisp, clear, authoritative voice bellowing out from behind his bushy Boer beard. He had been a voortrekker, on the Great Trek itself, a pioneer. That is why I chose the railways as a career I suppose. There was no new territory to trek into but the spirit of the voortrekker lived on within my breast. I needed to be forever on the move.

I seem to recall that he first spoke those words to me on a Sunday when I was aged about six or perhaps seven. We had been reading the Ten Commandments and I had reached the second one. Thou shalt not make unto thee any graven image. I had questioned it, not because I thought that it was wrong – how could one even doubt the Holy Word of God? – but because I didn't understand what a graven image was. I thought it was to do with graves you see, but graves don't have images on them, or at least, not good Reformist graves. My grandfather though, he only heard the doubt and so he took it on himself to remove that doubt. 'Wilhelm, it is not important that you understand; some rules we never can understand. They seem to us to be pointless, or even counterproductive. But that does not matter. Those rules come from God, either directly or indirectly, and so we obey them. Question rules and break them and all that is left is chaos, anarchy, sin. Look at the blacks with their mud huts, their fornication and their dirt: that is what happens to a people with no rules.'

And because I loved my grandfather and because I feared the chaos that I saw every time I passed through a native village then, from that day forward I always obeyed the rules without question.

---

I like the railways. I like the singing of the wheels on the iron road. I like the breeze in my face and the clatter of the carriages as they traverse the points. I like the unknown towns and the distant horizon. I like the drums echoing in the night from the native villages and I like the smell of coal smoke whenever we plunge into a tunnel.

All of these things I like, but what I do not like are kaffirs with ideas above their station. Kaffirs in general I can cope with, but not those who think they are something else. Those who break the rules ordained by God.

Just my luck then that I got one that day. On the very day that I was feeling ill from a cold and worrying about little Anneke who had come down with a fever in the morning and whose health has not been robust ever since she was born this twelve months past.

So, with the weight of illness, doctor's fees and fatigue on my brain, what better time for me to meet an idiot?

Harrison brought him to my attention. Michael Harrison is a British merchant who has the ear of the Governor. He takes the Durban to Jo'burg train every week as he has business interests in both cities. Plus, he tips generously. He can afford to. So, imagine my horror when he comes to my office and informs me that there is a kaffir in his compartment. I had not checked the carriage of course; with First Class one generally does not have to, but when I went down there, lo and behold, there it was, an Indian dressed up in a Savile Row suit, smiling his stupid smile and telling me there has been some mistake.

'I am a lawyer, sir, going to a case in Johannesburg.'

A lawyer. Who ever heard of a kaffir lawyer?

'I have a ticket, sir, a first-class ticket. I ordered it through the mail.

His voice was whiny and sycophantic. The same stupid voice as all Indians. I told him to move but he continued to protest. 'But sir...'

His voice though, I did not hear. Instead only that of my grandfather rang in my head. 'Question rules and break them and all that is left is chaos, anarchy, sin.' If I allowed this one, there would be another and another and another.

Five minutes later we pulled into Pietermaritzburg and there we threw him off the train.

And, of course, that was the beginning. I did not realise it at the time, but later it became clear. That Indian lawyer really was what he had said and within months he was all over the news, proclaiming all races are equal and breaking every law going. His star was on the rise.

And while his rose, mine fell. Anneke, darling Anneke died in her sleep and, a year later, so did Gaabrielle giving birth to my son. Suddenly this land that my grandfather and father had tried to civilise held no affections for me, instead it was only a graveyard of hard memories being weakened at the foundations by men like that lawyer on the train. In my dreams I saw only grinning blacks and the inevitable rot and decay of all that we had built. This was not a country to grow old in, not a country to raise my son in.

And so, we left, headed east. I am a voortrekker, born of voortrekkers. I need to be moving, to be exploring a new world, not rotting in a graveyard.

But that kaffir on the train, you ask me, do I regret throwing him off and, by doing so, changing history? This is something I have tossed over in my mind countless times, indeed, but at the end of the day, my grandfather's words always come back to me.

Question rules and break them and all that is left is chaos, anarchy, sin.

And a man who abandons his ancestors; well, what kind of a man is that?

# Part 4

## Nottingham, UK
## 2018

I like that girl. I really do. There is something of me in her, yes indeed, our personalities are not so different. And our situations too. She will not accept the lot that she is given in life, the role that society tells her that she must play. Now – she is so young after all – she does not realise this fully, but she will. She is awakening to the fact that freedom is there to be taken, that what they tell us we must be, we do not have to be. Madiba, the hero that freed a people, once said that when a man is denied the right to live the life he believes in, he has no choice but to become an outlaw. She is now the outlaw, as was I. Soon she will break those chains. I remember when I did.

Jo'burg in those days was a halcyon place. After the long dark night of apartheid, the bright dawn of the New South Africa was shining. We believed that anything was possible. Looking back today, over two decades on, what with all the corruption, Mr. Zuma now languishing in prison and the blacks still poor whilst the whites are still rich, it seems laughable, but it is true. We had united and had lost our chains. The future was ours to take.

Of course, I walked into the city a naïve country bumpkin. I did not know who I was, let alone what was the world. I had done what I had been told to do: studied hard, worked hard and married a girl from my town who did not appal me. I believed I was happy because I had done what they told me would make a man happy. And as a reward for being that good little boy, my boss sent me to the big city to work for a fortnight at the head office there. I was in awe. I had never been further than Pietermaritzburg in my life and here I was, being sent to this vast metropolis. I stepped down onto the platform at Park Station and my eyes were agog: the place was huge! Line after line, more than ten definitely, trains going here and there, people waiting, boarding and rushing about. I wandered through into the vast foyer, as huge has twenty houses and then onto the street, rows of minibuses, a cacophony of people and traffic, buildings higher than any tree and a thousand smells assaulting my nostrils. It was unbelievable, overpowering... and I loved it.

The work placement went well. I was industrious then as I am now. But back then I was obedient and unquestioning too. I performed the tasks that I was given, and they liked my manner. I made friends too among these strange, worldly-wise city folk. Jacob was the first of these.

He knew before I did. I am sure of it. He could sniff out those invisible signals. He had learnt to do so over a long period. Later I heard what it had been like before Madiba came to power. The prison sentences, beatings, condemnation from a society that already exiled you because of your skin. Living like that and you must surely develop a sixth sense. Jacob had.

He suggested that we go out for some drinks on the Saturday and he took me to the fashionable Melrose District. We went to a couple of normal places first and then he took me into Ratz. I was later to become a regular in the place, but I have never forgotten that first night. Men dancing with men, women kissing women, men living as women. Something stirred in me. Strange as this might sound, but in an instant, I knew.

Like Paul in the Street Called Straight, the scales fell from my eyes.

They sent me to Jo'burg regularly for I was successful there and head office liked me. Jacob liked me even though we never became lovers. Once or twice a month I would ride the rails to the great city and he and I would party like it was 1999. Freedom was still new and fresh, both personally and nationally.

Or at least, it was there. Back in Ixopo though, nothing had changed. People lived as they always had and Miriam was always there when I got home. She loved me just as much as she had done when we wed and she treated me with her fine cooking and her advances in the bedroom. But whilst she had not altered, I was no longer the Desmond that she had married.

And being unable to both satisfy her and explain to her, ripped me up inside. Every Sunday we sat on the polished pews of St. Lawrence's and she was still the same pious, godly soul I had met at college. I though, I was nothing more than a liar and a grievous sinner.

On more than one occasion I stood on the edge of the railway platform as a long freight train approached, intending to make that final step in the journey of life, to end the pain and the angst. Each time though, I drew back, not through fear but from something else. Something that, even today, I cannot put my finger on. An unfulfilled destiny perhaps?

And so, I prayed for change but no change appeared and instead the only consolation came in Ratz and Babylon.

And in the arms of Luke.

---

Luke. Luke. Luke. I run his name over and over again in my mind and love it more each time I do so. Our attraction was instant, and Jacob understood. Still, it took three meetings before went back to his place. After the act, we lay together and he said to me, 'I know this sounds crazy, but I do not feel that I am with a man with you; you are the Grace that you dress up as, not the Desmond that your ID card tells me you are. I am meant to be gay but how can I be gay when the one I love is a woman?'

'Do not try to understand,' I replied.

He was white and he was English. He had not inherited any of the hatred of the Boers and instead saw me not as a kaffir but a person. And not just a person, but as the woman that I now realised I truly was internally and had to become externally.

But to do that I needed to leave my past behind.

I knew that I was going to change the day that I lay with Luke. The morning when I woke up in his arms after making that monumental decision, my first infidelity, I knew. But knowing and knowing that you know are two different things if that makes any sense. It probably doesn't. it didn't to me either. But from that day on life could not continue as it had. Desmond had died; I had killed him.

Luke and I grew closer and he told me about what doctors could do these days. I couldn't afford it of course, but he promised to help. What about Miriam though, my innocent angel in the house? How could I hurt her so? Desmond, though, had died, and so she had to mourn. And that would not be possible if she knew where the body that once housed him was still living. The sky was thundery when she waved me off from Ixopo railway station, thinking I would only be gone for two days. The rain that lashed down from the gods was only a shadow of the tears that formed rivulets on my cheeks.

I will not tell you all the details. The medical procedures with long, complicated names, the pain both mental and physical. But slowly, over three years, Grace was born. Luke got her a new job and became her partner. Neither of us had been happier in our lives. We were as children and Jo'burg was our playground. And like childhood, we lived in a simple bliss.

Childhood though, must end, as the real world becomes apparent. And although Desmond was long dead, his shadow hung over us. It always would whilst we lived in South Africa. Luke longed to return home and I wished to join him... as his wife. But my old shadow Desmond was married and we shared an identity card.

Never have I felt fear like on that trip back to Ixopo, my first in five years. Never have I felt trepidation like I did when I knocked on the door of our old home. And never have I felt relief when that knock went unanswered. I did not have to face her and admit my deception! I could skulk away like a fox in the night. I posted the letter of explanation and apology along with the divorce papers and then slid away, back to the comforting cocoon of the railway carriage.

God, though, doth move in mysterious ways and who should I meet by chance on Pietermaritzburg station, tired, smiling and unsuspecting? Her radiance and goodness shone through and I talked to her as I have always longed to. As myself. As a woman.

And I know she understood.

---

I am older now, a woman in a far-off land, my husband in his grave and my living now earned through a quiet little job in the local library. Aside from missing Luke every day, I am happy. I lose myself in books and immerse myself in the petty yet fascinating lives of the lenders who come in. Lenders like this girl. As I said, I like her, I really do. There is something of me in her. Yes indeed, our personalities are not so different. And our situations too. But we have one crucial difference between us: age. I have lived the life, fought the good fight and now approach the quieter time in life. For her, it is all just beginning. She is just discovering the world and her eyes are as round as mine were when I stepped off the train in Jo'burg.

In every story you can see a theme. Several basic plots run through them all, boy meets girl, hero defeats the dragon. And the same characters too. The heroes are young. They are good but they need knowledge. And always there is an older, wiser figure to provide it for them. Perhaps, in the tale of Someya Sayyid, that wise old sage is me. Amazing Grace!

She told me today of a friend from school who had committed suicide. She was aghast and judgemental. 'It is a terrible sin,' she told me. 'The Prophet said that whoever throws himself down from a mountain and kills himself will be throwing himself down in the Fire of Hell for ever and ever.' I put my arm on her shoulder and said softly, 'Maybe so, maybe not, I cannot say. But, believe me, anyone in that position is only to be pitied. Their life must be tortured beyond all imagining. If you come across someone like that, talk to them and, however terrible their story, listen all the way through. You may save their life in more way than one.'

Who knows if that advice will ever be of use, or even listened to? One never can tell. Instead, like the farmer in the parable, all we can do is sow the seed, not knowing which ground it will fall on.

Ah, it is four-thirty, we close in half an hour. I must go now; I need to check the kids' section. They pull all in the books in and out and they are always put back in the wrong place. Excuse me, I have a job to do...

# Part 5

*Hong Kong*
*1949*

He took his passport from the official and looked at the stamp.

IMMIGRATION DEPARTMENT
HONG KONG
ENTRY
19 MAR 1949

There it was emblazoned in still-damp ink. Hong Kong. He was back. Those nightmares of eight years before were now just that. Fading dreams, half-remembered horrors. Order and normality had returned.

The realisation had begun when the plane had started its descent, down and down steeply, as if one were heading into the very mountainside itself and then banking sharply to the right, so close to the apartments that you could see what they were cooking for breakfast, before screeching to a halt on the treacherous tarmac of Kai Tak Airport. Nowhere on the planet announces itself as dramatically as Hong Kong, that outpost of civilisation in the east, buildings clinging to lush green slopes, the Chinese dragon mated with the British bulldog. Heady, intoxicating, vibrant, there wasn't any place on earth that he loved more.

Why then, did his heart feel so heavy as he stepped out of the terminal building and hailed a cab?

Why was he so petrified as to what he might find?

---

Eight years earlier...

Sunlight streamed in through the open window illuminating the curves of your body as you lay there on the bed, the mesmerising fall and rise of your breasts as you journeyed through the realm of dreams. I sat and watched you for how long I cannot say, marvelling at your smooth, silky skin, your lustrous black tresses and the lids that protect the ebony pearls of your eyes. And as I watched you sleep, I wondered. At times you looked like a child almost, yet from another angle you were a full woman with a look of wisdom and experience that far exceeded my own loathsome lot. You were a riddle wrapped in a mystery inside an enigma, yet still I loved you fiercely. Mei Ling will always remain part-mystery to me, there is something in your character that I would never fathom or understand and yet, somehow, that did not bother me. No matter whether I understood you fully or not, I loved you completely. You accepted me for who I was; did not look askance at my limp nor made fun of my laboured breathing. Girls of my own race laughed at my disabilities; you simply did not see them.

But as I thought those thoughts, a dark cloud crossed my mind, a cloud in the shape of my father. 'Have you been with your yellow whore today?' he'd sneer. Why did he have to be so bigoted? He had left South

Africa behind yet brought his homeland's odious prejudices with him. I thought of his threat to cut me out of his will unless I dumped you.

But I would not discard you and you were no whore. Mei Ling, you were my life and my father would have to learn to accept that. One way or another.

You stirred, opened your almond eyes lazily and smiled. 'I dream you are by my side and now I wake up my dream come true and I thank Guan Yin,' you said.

I leaned over and kissed you on the lips and wished that the moment could last for all eternity.

---

Daniel Wong stared back at him without a smile on his lips. 'I will be straight with you, Mr. van den Ouden,' he said in his Cantonese-accented English. 'The chances of success are not high. Mei Ling is a common name and these photographs are not very clear. Plus, it is true that many people died during the Japanese occupation. I saw bodies piled up in the streets, victims of the hunger and brutality. I must warn you of the possibility that your Mei Ling was one of those bodies.'

'I am aware of the possibility, but I wish for you to search for her anyhow. I must find out what happened to her.'

'Mr. van den Ouden, if anyone in Hong Kong can find her, it is Daniel Wong, Private Detective. Please return here in a week's time and I will update you on my progress.'

---

Eight years before...

We knew they were coming. Everybody knew. They had been ploughing through Asia for months, years even, coming ever nearer. Nothing that stood in their way could stop them. They ripped through China and Indochina like a whirlwind and then cast their eyes on us Europeans. On

193

the 10th they sunk two battleships out near Malaya, and then they turned on us. And with our army and navy already stretched by the Nazis, there was little we could do.

I wanted to stay and fight. I pleaded to be allowed to do so, but what use is a lame epileptic to the military? I was to be evacuated with the women, children and elderly. The thought of leaving both the city and the woman that I loved tore through my heart like a hurricane, leaving me an empty shell.

Confusion and terror reigned. People were packing small travelling cases whilst overhead planes roared. You could hear the distant rattle of machine gun fire from the mainland. People filled the streets, making their way to the port but I turned the other way. 'Where are you going?' my father putting his hand on my shoulder to stop me.

'I have to get her; I cannot leave her here?'

'Get who?'

'You know who. I cannot leave her. The Japs will...'

'They will do nothing. They are sneaky yellow shits just like she is, like all those Orientals are. Leave her; she is nothing. A white man like you should not be seen with a yellow bitch like her!'

'Will you never leave your racist attitudes behind you? After all these years and still you have not learned!'

'God made the races separate; they should not mix. That is God's law. Mongrels are worthless creatures, accepted by none and that is all you could ever produce!'

'I love her and she loves me! And if we ever had a child I would love it too! I will go back for her!'

'Go back then, but you won't find her. Your whore has left.'

'What do you mean, left?'

'I paid her. I told her that you'd died. The bomb that fell on Lockhart Road yesterday. She spent last night crying at the scene. She has mourned you and moved away.'

I realised what he had done, how he repulsed me, and how hopeless it was. Even if I looked, she would not be found. My own father had destroyed my life's happiness in an instant with his hate and prejudices. I looked into his face and asked a simple question:

'Why?'

'I am a voortrekker. You are my son. A voortrekker must move on continually. A voortrekker does not mix with kaffir. A voortrekker only takes his own kind with him.'

'I am no son of yours,' I replied.

I sat for an hour in that room, not caring if the Japs came or not. In the end the soldiers had to drag me out.

---

Following my departure from Hong Kong, the hardships continued. We were crammed in like sardines and, since the ship had not been fumigated, conditions were not good to say the least. Perhaps because of this, but more due to the fact of being separated from Mei Ling, I developed a fever and drifted in and out of consciousness for the entire voyage, a voyage plagued by bad weather and the risk of attack by submarines. By the time we made landfall at Brisbane, I had lost three stone and was a shadow of the man I had been previously.

But in Australia I was well looked after and, after some time, my body recovered even if my heart did not. My father came to visit me several times, but I refused to speak with him. Indeed, I have not done so to this day and never shall until he at least apologises, an eventuality that I doubt I shall ever witness.

Stubborn old fool.

Eventually it was decided that us evacuees were to return to Britain, and we sailed up the Clyde on a really cold May morning in 1942. Never have I felt so alone and despondent. Before me I only saw exile from the woman I loved, the rape of my home city by the Japs, a father who had ruined my life and grey skies thick with Nazi bombers overhead. Back then hope was wholly absent.

Thankfully, there is at least a glimmer now.

---

This is the place. The place that David Wong private detective agency have informed me is where a Mei Ling who might be her resides. Standing here, scared almost to ring the bell, I survey what I see before me. A battered door adorned with peeling paint, my heart still pounding after climbing four flights of stairs, the smells of cooked rice, cabbage, incense and laundry wafting into my nostrils and the faint cries of a dozen babies from a score of surrounding apartments. Is this it? Is this where you have ended up my love? In this squalid hole, a pale imitation of the splendour in which we marinated. My love! What has become of you? How could I have left you? Will you ever forgive me?

I ring the bell and wait. For a second, two seconds, three, four, an age. Silence. Only the babies wail in the background. You are not here. You are gone. Wong was wrong. Mei Ling did not survive the war. She was murdered by the Japs, starved in some camp, beaten, abused…

A sound! A creak on the boards. Hope?

The door rattles and opens a crack. 'Shénme?' says a voice. Not her voice. This voice is cracked and dry; that of a stranger.

'Mei Ling,' I say. 'I have come to see Mei Ling. I was told that she lives here.'

The door opens to reveal a crone. 'Mei Ling, missa?' she asks.

'Mei Ling,' I confirm.

She shrieks in Cantonese. Others shriek in return. All is lost. I see your corpse by the side of the road, emaciated, another victim of Jap brutality. But then, in an instant, that vision of hell disintegrates. It is you. Older, more worn and tired, but you nonetheless. Heaven's doors open. I smile. 'Mei Ling, I did not die,' I say.

A smile spreads across your face too, but you do not touch me. Instead you turn away and disappear. What does this mean? I stand confused on the threshold, unable to move forward or back. Where have you gone? Why have you gone? 'Mei Ling!' I call, desperate.

You reappear followed by a small child. He stares at me with wide eyes. Has he ever seen a white man before? He clings to you, afraid, unsure.

Then I notice.

Those eyes are blue.

'His name is Peter,' you say. 'He is our son.'

# Part 6

*Shanklin, Isle of Wight*
*2018*

That day he went to Shanklin.

Thinking about it logically, could he have gone anywhere else? After all, in a strange way, psychologically, was that not where it all started?

Shanklin, the small seaside town that he had not set foot in ever since that idyllic family holiday, fifty-nine years ago. The holiday that would, in a roundabout way, change his life. The holiday that had created the situation he was in now.

He walked off the Wightlink ferry at Ryde Pier Head and crossed over to the railway station where the little red train, ex-tube stock like he had travelled on as a boy, was waiting. As it was out-of-season the carriage was largely empty. There was only one other occupant in fact, a young Muslim lady with a scarf tightly cocooning her head. There hadn't been any Muslims on the train back in 1959. She was looking at her phone; he looked out of the window.

He got off at Shanklin and walked towards the beach. Despite his age, he had retained his mobility and was thankful for it. He saw so many people, half his age even, using sticks or mobility scooters. For the first time in a week he felt lucky.

He made his way through B&B-blessed streets, a hundred Vacancies signs on show and stopped briefly outside The Chestnuts where he had stayed all those years before. Then he moved on.

At the Eastcliff Promenade he stopped again and savoured the view. He leant on the fence and looked down upon the beach and Esplanade far below and he remembered. He remembered her golden hair, he remembered their walk on that beach, he remembered…

He remembered her leaving.

He turned right onto the clifftop walk. There was no fence there.

And no people.

Taking a deep breath, he strengthened his resolve. With a silent prayer to a God that he had never really believed in and always neglected, he stepped towards the edge. Even the sight made him dizzy. But he had no choice. He took another step forward and…

'Excuse me, mister, excuse me?'

What? Who? He stepped back, opened his eyes and turned around. There was a girl there, an Asian girl, her jet-black hair blowing in the wind. She had kind eyes.

'You were thinking of suicide, weren't you?'

What could he say? What could he do? Why did she have to turn up now?

'I asked you a question.'

He nodded.

'It's not worth it, you know?'

'You don't know me; you don't know my life.'

'Tell me then.'

---

'Last week, Friday actually. There was a ring on my doorbell and when I opened it, I was most surprised to discover two police constables standing there. "Can I help you, officers?" I asked them. "Are you Peter van den Ouden?" one of them asked me. "Yes," I replied. "Peter van den Ouden, I am arresting you on suspicion of the crime of rape of a minor."'

She stiffened involuntarily. He noticed it and his monologue trailed off. She'd asked him to be honest, but people cannot handle honesty. The charges were too despicable. He was too despicable. He began to back away.

Her head was churning. Rape. Minor. What the hell was this? This was beyond sin, it was so haram that words could not describe it. Throw himself off the cliff. No wonder. She could not listen; she had brothers and sisters, cousins… But then the words came back to her. Grace's words: "Man is made in the image of God. God means 'good'. What that means is that there is some good in all of us. Your job is to find that good and work with it. Forget about the rest: it is irrelevant."

'Wait!' she said.

He stopped.

'You haven't finished your story, Peter.'

He looked at her. Shock emanated from his whole face. She realised. No one had ever listened before. Her stomach churched at what she was about to hear but she knew that she needed to hear it because he needed to say it.

'The police... they were in my house. I...'

'How did you feel, Peter?'

His face relaxed. His heart relaxed. Who was this girl? This stranger? 'I felt... I... in an instant my whole life was ruined. One minute I was looking forward to living out my days in a genteel and pleasant retirement; the next all I have to look forward to are four walls and a window with bars on it and shame... shame.'

'You don't know that. They may not find you guilty.'

He looked at her and she knew. The churning intensified. 'Even if you do go to prison, that doesn't mean that suicide is a better option. You can study in prison, read, relax.'

'The prison maybe, maybe I could cope with. But the shame, now that is something else. You wouldn't understand it.'

She thought. She remembered the course that Grace had recommended to her on dealing with people contemplating suicide. The course that had made her notice him in the first place. "Find some common ground, work on it. Create empathy." Empathy. Shame. Yes, she could empathise with that. This was home territory for her! 'Wouldn't I, Peter? Now you are the one talking about a life you know nothing about. As a young Muslim woman I know all about shame. I too have a story to tell.'

'I'm sorry, I...'

'Let me tell it to you. Look, there is a café down there, by the dinosaur crazy golf. Let me tell it to you over a cup of tea.'

---

Rain had started to spit so they sat inside. Peter looked out through the window and remembered that day all those years before. It had been raining then. When she had gone.

'And now, when I finally plucked up the courage, you came; a girl I've never even seen before in my life.'

'But you have seen me before,' she replied. Peter's stomach leapt. He had not realised that he had spoken those words out loud.

'I didn't... when? I mean, when have we met before?'

'On the train coming here. You were sitting in the same carriage as me. I noticed then how miserable you looked as you gazed out of the window. Like a man with the weight of the world on his shoulders. When we both got off at Shanklin and you started to walk towards the clifftop, I decided to follow you. A gut feeling.'

'But the girl on the train. She had a scarf on.'

It's in my bag; we call it our "hijab". "My hijab is my crown, my hijab is my modesty, my hijab is my ticket to heaven. My hijab is my dignity, my respect and my honour and I will never trade it for this temporary world."'

'Excuse me?'

'We used to have to recite that bullshit every day at school, the Jamia al-Hudaa Residential College for Girls. And I believed it, truly believed. Girls should be modest and pious, girls are pearls to be protected and cherished, lest they should bring shame upon their family. Oh yes, I know all about shame!'

'But you took it off now.'

'Yes, for the first time ever in public. Like you I've been working myself up for something. I got to that clifftop, in a town where no one knows me but where I went on a family holiday when I was twelve, the year I became a woman, the time my dad told me I should put it on. Here was the last place where I had my hair free and here is the first place it is free again. Anyway, that is my story; what's yours?'

Peter stared into his teacup. No, he couldn't tell her. It was too embarrassing. Too awful.

'I'm a stranger Peter, what does it matter what you tell a stranger?'

He nodded and began: 'I also came here on a family holiday but I was thirteen, not twelve. We stayed just up there in a place called The Chestnuts. It was a glorious hot summer and I was happy. I was still a child, well, almost. But then she came. She arrived two days after us with her parents. Her name was Millie and she came from Haywards Heath. We were the same age. She had light golden hair and beautiful blue eyes. She stirred something in me that I had never felt before. I, who had always shied away from girls, instead felt drawn towards her... and she to me. We became inseparable. We went to the beach together, climbed the cliffs, played on the penny arcades and... kissed. It was magical, like I had gone to heaven. I told her that I loved her and that we should get married when we were old enough. She told me that she felt the same way.'

He stopped and stared out of the window. Then slowly he pointed towards the far end of the beach. 'Over there, that is where we pledged ourselves. But then... then the next day it rained and she was gone. The landlady said that they had had to return because her grandmother had fallen ill and could die. That day though, I believe I was the one who died. Something inside of me went... I was never the same again.'

Outside the rain had stopped and rays of sunshine had started to push through the clouds.

'All my life, even to this day, I never got over it. That sounds stupid I know, but it is true. All my life I was chasing Millie. She was my girl, the one I was destined to be with, alas, fate had cut us short. But as I grew older, it became a problem. When I was fifteen, liking girls a couple of years younger was no problem, but when you are twenty or thirty or forty and the only girl who makes you feel alive is thirteen, still largely a child, then...'

He was silent again, staring into the teacup again, immersed in the past again.

'I only succumbed once. She was a friend's daughter. The guy was named Colin Bartlett; we read History at Durham together and stayed close. When I was about thirty, I started babysitting his kids when he and his wife wanted to go to a film or theatre show. Their daughter was twelve, only a little younger than Millie had been. They looked similar too. What I did was wrong. I told her that if she ever said anything her dad would be very angry as he was good friends with me. She never did; not until now.'

'It was brave of you to tell me all that,' said the Asian girl, recalling the instructions on the course. Get them to talk. Positive reinforcement. 'Thank you.'

'You were just as brave with the whole scarf thing!'

'It feels good you know. I feel like I am no longer living a lie; I am the real Someya now who wants to walk around without her hair covered, talking to a strange white man if she wishes, experiencing the world.'

'Enough of the strange white man! I'm half Asian myself. My mother was Chinese. When my parents got together it caused an awful fuss. They didn't look on race the same way then as we do now.'

'So maybe my rebellion will become less impressive too as the years pass?'

'You can hope so. But you are right, one should be honest. I will plead Guilty and damn the consequences. You are not the only one who has lived a lie. I have done so for much longer and, let me tell you, it can eat you up inside.'

They both smiled and looked at the sun outside.

'Turned out nice," said Peter. "How can I ever repay you Miss...?'

'Someya, Someya Sayyid. And how can you repay me? You don't need to. Repay someone else instead. That is how the world works...'

# Part 7

## Changsha, China
## 2018

It calls to her. Even after all these years. There, every night, she sees it in her mind's eye. Waiting, tempting, delectable and enticing. 'Nkosazana, come to me! Let your lips touch me, envelope me, devour me!' She shakes the image from her head, knowing that she will never truly be free and shifts her mind back to the page before her eyes. Will Prince Andrew marry Natasha? She hopes that he does, with all of his heart as he is such a good man and she is a lovely sweet girl. But then the age difference could prove problematic and where will that leave Pierre. Ach, that man! His marriage to Helene is nothing more than a sham and whilst she is undoubtedly more beautiful than I will ever be, she can be such a zulinghu. Of course, it must be said that he is a strange man but his heart is in the right place, is it not? Ach, what will happen!

The bottle has gone from her mind.

---

It has been ten years now. Ten whole years. A full decade since a drop of alcohol passed her lips. Haleluya! Mdumise uYehova! But still she knows. One drop more and it could take over again. Once an alcoholic, always an alcoholic. That is what they say. And yet, she was not always that way.

It was Desmond of course. Desmond, Desmond, Desmond. That man who is gone yet also still here. Dead, yet alive. Resurrected, reincarnated, whatever. The man she hates and yet also loves. Back then she only loved him. Way back then, in the concrete precincts of Ixopo High School, the air thick with hormones, her dressed in the regulation navy skirt, black socks and sky-blue shirt. She loved him even then. He was so kind and open, a boy that you could talk to like a girlfriend rather than one of those macho louts who played football every break. Inside she laughs. The signs were always there, but she never saw them. Instead, all she saw was a boy who saw her as the person she was, not fat and ugly and dull like the rest of the world saw. He gave her time when the others passed her by. Was it any wonder that she latched onto him, became addicted?

Addicted. Yes, addicted. It sounds strange to call a relationship by that word, but that is what it was, an addiction. She sees that now with the benefit of the years. She became addicted and they got married. And all was good. In a way. On the surface.

And then he disappeared.

The drinking started before then of course. When he went away to the city on business and she was alone in that unfriendly house with only housework for company, on those evenings the bottle of mampoer, bought from the local shebeen queen and kept under the sink, would be brought out and she would pour a glass. Or two. Never so much, just a little. To banish the shadows.

But when he left for the city and never came back, sending only that spartan message as a goodbye, then those shadows lengthened and that glass or three was never enough to banish them. Especially at night.

Those days were painful. She still went out and about, continuing as if things were as things should be. 'Morning, Nkosazana!', 'How are you,

Nkosazana?'; 'My husband, yes, he is away in the city on business again, that is why you have not seen him. No, he is very well, well indeed. All is well with us, Mdumise uYehova!' It was only after three months that she stopped pretending but by then it had become intolerable.

To her face they acted like angels. That zulinghu Lindiswa Jan and that bhentse emfene Mihlali Ndamase. 'Hello, Nkosazana Mzamane, how are you today? We do so hope that you are well?' But behind her back they would be whispering, 'Ach, look at her, that Miriam Mzamane with the big ngqundu! She is so fat and ugly, she could not even keep her man! That woman could not satisfy even a mouse like him so he left her for a zulinghu in the city!' Yes, she knew what they were like. Devils!

But the mampoer was different. It did not gossip nor spread lies. It only numbed and helped her to forget... and sleep. But, like them, it also had two faces. That she discovered as time passed and all her friends and family stayed away and the work she relied on dried up. The other face of the bottle left her more alone than ever, increasing her reliance as the sun rose on each new damned day.

---

A voice crackles over the tannoy: 'Xiànzài jiējìn wǔ hào píngtái de huǒchē shì Guǎngzhōu de shíqī diǎn èrshí fēn.' She is jerked back into the present. She does not understand it all, but she picks out the bits that matter: 'huǒchē' is 'train', 'shíqī diǎn èrshí fēn' is '17:20' and 'Guǎngzhōu' is, well, 'Guangzhou'. In short, her train is arriving.

It is amazing just how much her life has changed from then, only ten years ago. From a monotonous hell of waking up each morning in that lonely house on the outskirts of Ixopo, dousing herself with mampoer to cope with the pain and passing out with only worse health and greater debts to show for it. And now what? Now she is standing on the pristine platform of Changsha's railway station after having secured the deal she came to get and returning home to her apartment in the sought-after district of Panyu, Guangzhou.

Her home, yes, you heard right. Guangzhou, not Ixopo. And not a bottle of mampoer (or any other liquor) in sight. Miriam Mzamane, no longer the grieving wife of the absent Desmond but instead the go-ahead real-estate agent with the best portfolio this side of Hong Kong.

---

I wonder about him you know. Sometimes, when I am lying alone in my bed, I wonder about my Desmond. I still love him in a way, even though he is gone. Well, sort-of gone. Is he happy now as her? Did that give him the peace that I could not? I hope so for it could not have been easy and if it did not work, then you cannot go back to what you were, eh? I like to think that he... she, is happy now, maybe sitting at home with a cup of rooibos tea and a book in her hand. Desmond... Grace, God be with you.

Of course, it was Desmond's fault in a way that my life went in that terrible direction, but, strangely, it was Grace to thank for pulling me out again. I read a book a couple of years ago about the Buddha and how he tried lots of different and crazy things – starving himself, begging and such like – to reach the answer and then, in the end, it just happened under the bodhi tree. I too tried different things. I realised after only a couple of years that the drinking was bad and could only end in a dark place. But nothing worked, nothing could fill that hole in my soul. And then, one day, on the station in Pietermaritzburg, I met Grace by chance and learned who my Desmond had become and why he had left me alone. In an instant the worries and the feelings of guilt and inadequacy disappeared. It made sense. And with that, nothing held me back.

Of course, it is much more complicated than that. I still longed for the mampoer just as I do today, but I developed ways to deal with that also. Strangely, they too came from Pietermaritzburg railway station. Some months after my meeting with Grace, I was approached by a foreigner, an Asian gentleman. 'Excuse me,' he said, 'but is this the platform for the train to Ixopo?' It was of course, and we began to talk. It turned out that he had travelled all the way from China to visited my hometown. 'But why?' I asked him. 'Because of the book,' he'd replied. 'Ixopo is the town of Stephen Kumalo, the hero of your country's greatest novel. I read this book when I was only a child and always dreamed to see this place.'

Of course, I knew that Cry, the Beloved Country was set in my town, but I had never read it. When I told the man, he could not believe what he heard and, do you know what, I felt ashamed. And so I borrowed a copy from the library and that night I began to read it and I fell in love all over again.

And while you can write with mampoer inside you, reading is not possible. It clouds the brain. And so, something had to give and, with time, it was the drink. And when I was free of drink, my life began anew: a fresh job, success and then, two years ago, moving to China.

Ach, my train is here now, the sleek coaches pulling in. Life is strange, is it not? Maybe I should have my ashes scattered on a railway station when I die. Those chance, brief encounters with Grace and that Chinese man turned my life around completely. It is only a shame that I did not meet someone here today, but they are less open and chatty in these parts than in Africa. And besides, who knows, maybe I shall meet someone on the train? Another chance encounter with a stranger. Yes indeed, that would be nice.

# Part 8

## Savile Town, West Yorkshire
## 2018

For over an hour after the appointment Sayyid did not move. He sat at the wheel of his Toyota Avensis and stared at the brick wall in front of him. His eyes were fixed and his mouth stayed silent. His mobile phone rang fourteen times yet he did not answer it. He could not.

When he eventually put the key into the ignition and turned it, the sun had begun to set. For the first time in over three decades he missed the maghrib prayer.

The following morning he went to the masjid. After the silent cocoon of the car, his home had been a riot of emotions. Tears and lamentations, raised voices, even accusations. For the first time in his life he envied those gorah who cared not for family and lived on their own in dingy flats or houses. The cacophony was excruciating. He was in the masjid not to pray but to escape.

'Why? Why?' Why?' he asked God, continually, repeatedly, like a stuck record.

Why indeed?

Had he not always lived within the precepts of his faith?

Had he not always recited the prayers?

Had he not always worked hard to support his family?

Had he not always protected his wives and children?

Had he not always given zakat?

Had he not made both the hajj and the umrah?

Had he not spread the deen?

Had he not done everything that had been asked of him?

Yet despite all that, God had visited all this on him. Yesterday, the worst day of his life. It had started badly. His daughter, Someya announcing that she had decided to take off her hijab. Nineteen years of Islamic upbringing and education and she was being seduced by the ways of the gorah the moment that she had entered that university. There had been an almighty row and she had banged the door and stormed out. It could not have got worse.

Except that it then did.

His appointment with Dr. Ranjit which he had almost clean forgotten about in all the furore, merely getting the results of some tests, and, within an hour his life had been ended. He remembers only snatches: 'Mr. Sayyid, sir, yes, I am sorry to say that it is cancer... you should have come earlier, when the symptoms first appeared... I know you are busy but... no, it is not operable now... too late... chemotherapy can slow things down... terminal... two years maximum...'

Why God, why? He tried to recall the story of the Prophet Ayub in the hope that it would give him strength but the strategy failed. After all, for that pious man 'We responded to him and removed what afflicted him of adversity'.

But who could remove his affliction?

In desperation, his head racing and aching as he leant again the pillar where he had prayed so many times over the years, he implored God to guide him.

And amidst the chaos in his head, a voice seemed to say, 'Consult the hadith.'

And so he got up and went over to the bookshelf at the back of the mosque and pulled out a Sahih Bukhari Collected Hadith which he opened at random and read what was written.

'Utlub il 'ilma wa law fis-Sin.

The Prophet (s) said, 'Seek knowledge even unto China,'

Seek knowledge?

Unto China?

What on earth could that mean?

He returned to his place, sat with his back against the pillar again, closed his eyes and meditated. He worked hard to clear his mind and to see what Allah was trying to tell him. What did this mean? What had it to do with him, a dying man?

We have only a short time on this earth, so we must use it wisely. That means to live piously, as I have done, but also to seek knowledge. And have I done that? I have read the Quran and sunnah of course, but beyond that? I am not so educated in a worldly way and, aside from my trips to Ayeesha's family in Pakistan and pilgrimages to the holy cities, I am not well-travelled. Work and raising a family have always been more important. Is that, therefore, what the Lord is telling me? I have a limited time left on this earth and one more task to perform? But why China?

He sat, thought and prayed for a long time but no answer came. Instead, the muezzin sounded for the dhuhr prayer. He waited as the imam came out in his robes and performed the actions in front of the mihrab. Sayyid followed every move, imploring God all the while for guidance. And when it was finished, the imam got up, saw him and came over. 'As-salamu alaykum, Brother Sayyid, I'm sorry, I did not see you there. I hope you are keeping well. By the way, we have a talk arranged this Friday after Jumma prayers; it's a respected sheikh from Malaysia who is coming to speak about the long and glorious history of the deen in the Far East. It's called 'Even unto China'. Would you mind spreading the word amongst the brothers on the ranks...?'

Now he knew.

---

Ayeesha had not reacted well when he had announced that he was going to China. He had explained about the hadith and his prayers but her faith, although profound, was more practical. 'That money was to pay for healthcare for my mother in Mirpur. Plus, we need a new boiler; the old one breaks down continually and it leaks terribly. What purpose is there in you going to China to do what exactly? Really Sayyid, it is too much. Zoya, thankfully, was as silent and accepting as ever but Someya, still shamefully parading around sans hijab, was surprisingly supportive. 'If that is what you need to do, papa, then you must do it.' Adam and Rashid merely shrugged their shoulders and left.

Three weeks later he boarded the plane to Beijing.

---

The day was hot and the large windows of the carriage refracted the light into even more intense heat. Although the uppermost portion of that window was open, it did little to dissipate the furnace. Sayyid was glad of his loose, cool clothing; yet another reason to rejoice in the truth of Allah's message, for had not He decreed the hijab for men and women alike and was it not cooling and healthy to wear?

His mind flitted back to his daughter's uncovered head as they waved him off at the airport and he boiled with anger. How dare she?!

It had been one thing deciding to travel to China yet quite another knowing how to do so. Take the weather for example: prior to his departure he'd not had a clue what the weather there would be like. Was it a hot country or a cold one, or just wet and miserable like England? He realised that this was a place that he knew absolutely nothing about, terra incognita. Eventually he'd packed both warm and cool outfits and now his case was weighed down with unnecessary coats, gloves and woolly hats. Astaghfirullah!

He felt the beads of sweat drip down his neck and onto his back. Such heat! Such a country!

Ever since his arrival it had overwhelmed him. So vast, so many people, all the same. They'd stared at him with his foreign clothes and lustrous beard. No men had beards here and he wondered if they could even grow them. Astaghfirullah! He'd taken a taxi into the centre of the city, mile after mile of skyscrapers and traffic jams. This place made Leeds or even London look like a village! No wonder they were taking over the world.

And even when he'd settled in his pre-booked hotel, things had been a struggle. He'd wandered through the streets looking for something to eat, but every restaurant had served meat – most likely pork and certainly not halal – and all the menus were in a strange alphabet that he couldn't understand and no one seemed to speak a word of English so he couldn't even ask if they had a vegetarian option. In the end of he had resorted to going into a convenience shop and buying several packets of crisps and chocolate bars before enjoying a sad and lonely meal in his dank and dingy hotel room. It was a new experience maybe, but hardly a pleasant one. Was this what was meant by seeking knowledge even unto China? Astaghfirullah!

And then there had been the itinerary. It was one thing buying a ticket to China but quite another knowing what to see and do once you're there. He recalled the lecture by the Malaysian sheikh that he'd attended. He had talked all about the mosques there, some of the oldest in the world, built by a Companion of the Prophet himself no less. There were two that he had gone on about: the Great Mosque of Xi'an and the Huaisheng Mosque in Guangzhou. That latter one had particularly intrigued him. It had been built in 627 by Sayid ibn Abi Waqas. Was his name not Sayyid too, and had his father not been called Waqas? Was this another sign? Thus, it was that he'd arranged a simple itinerary: from Beijing straight to Xi'an, then down to Guangzhou, then back up to Beijing and home. Nice and easy. Astaghfirullah! Why had he never checked how far those short distances on the map actually were?!

His eyes closed as he thought back over the previous days. To be fair, he had enjoyed Xi'an. It was a pleasant and interesting city, girded with ancient walls and full of old buildings. Most of them were Buddhist temples which had looked interesting from the outside, but Sayed was unsure about entering. Was it haram to knowingly go into a sanctuary where false idols are worshipped? He'd always warned his kids about setting foot inside a church back home and yet the blasphemies of Buddhism far exceeded those of the Christians who at least believed in all the prophets and the One God, albeit in a very mixed up way. So, in the end, he'd walked past and contented himself with more secular entertainments.

Another pleasant factor had been the presence of many Muslim restaurants. It was true that the food was strange to his palate, but he was assured that it was halal. Of course, whether it was, was another matter; back home in Dewsbury there had been a furore and an intensive campaign (which he had played a leading role in) over butchers and eateries that had claimed to be halal when, in fact, they did not meet all the proscribed standards. Were these places of the same ilk? It was possible but, faced with the alternative diet of crisps and chocolate bars which now caused bile to rise in his throat at even the thought, Sayed took the risk and dined out.

The Great Mosque too had caused mixed emotions. It was a beautiful place, yes, and intriguing, but to him it just did not feel like a mosque. True, there were quotes from the Quran displayed on the walls in beautiful calligraphy, but he felt like he were in an alien sanctuary, it looked more like one of those Buddhist temples than any mosque he had ever entered. It may have been Islam but it was not his Islam and he did not feel comfortable praying in there in amongst those small Chinamen with the embroidered white skullcaps and clean-shaven faces, men from another world whose way of life bore little relation to his own...

'Well this is so typical, do you not think?'

Sayyid was jerked awake by a loud voice right by his ear. His opened eyes were confronted by a vision, a most unexpected vision. A big, black vision.

She smiled a smile of white pearls. 'I swear to you, they see a foreigner and so they put them next to the other foreigner. This is always the way in China. This is the foreigner compartment now, ha!'

The voice was African. She was uncomfortably close to him. At Xi'an the bunk opposite to his own had been empty; now it was very full.

'So, tell me now please, what is your name?'

'Muhammed Sayyid, sister, and yours?'

'Miriam Mzamane at your service.'

She held out a plump hand.

'Sister, I am sorry, I cannot...'

'Why? You will not shake the hand of me when offered in friendship? Is it because I am black? Are you afraid to pollute your Indian skin with that of the negro?'

'No, it is not that; it is...'

But she never heard his explanation. Instead she burst out into a peal of laughter which caused a passing Chinese mother and child to stare into their berth with shock.

'Do not worry Brother Sayyid. I am from South Africa and we have many Muslims there. I was friends with a few myself. You do not shake the hand of a woman you are not related to, am I right?'

'Yes, sister, that is the case.'

'And it is because the contact may be construed as sexual, yes?'

'Yes.'

'Well, do not worry. I am not interested in that kind of thing, not at my age.' She winked. 'Orange?'

'Excuse me?'

'Orange? Do you want one? Here; they are very sweet. I picked them up in the market this morning.'

She proffered the fruit and he took it, his fingers brushing hers momentarily, the rule broken.

He had not been in the mood for a conversation, but with Miriam Mzamane there was no choice. She had come to chat and that was that.

'It is always the case; every time I am on the train, these Chinese are putting me next to a foreigner. You will never be accepted here, do you know that, never. You look different and that is that. To them you and me, we are the same.'

Looking at her, Sayyid did not feel particularly the same. However, he felt compelled to say something. 'We are all loved by God.'

'That is true, yes indeed. All children of God. Haleluya! Mdumise uYehova! But when I came here, the whole us and them thing, it bothered me. You know, I thought that they were horrible people, racists you know. They stared at me in the street. It upset me. That was partly what I had left South Africa to escape, the racism and other prejudices. In South Africa you see everything through those lens, the lens of racism and prejudice. Or at least you do if you are a person of colour as we both are. But here, after a while, I began to realise; they were racist, yes, but not in a nasty way.'

'How can racism not be nasty?'

'It is nasty when you look at the person who is different and look down on them or hate them. But when you look at them because they are different and wonder what they are like, then that is what I call a curious racism and to me that is fine. People stare at me because maybe they have never seen a black man or woman before. They like to feel my hair because it is wiry. There is no harm. Coming here taught me something.'

'It taught you what?'

'That I too had prejudices, not just those who discriminated against me. I saw everything in terms of people judging or attacking me; the Chinese taught me something else; that curiosity is not a sin and that sometimes I need to view things differently. Like it says in the Bible, the scales fell from my eyes.'

Sayyid gazed out of the window. The train was passing row upon row of towering apartment blocks, each identical, each more than twenty storeys high. A forest of concrete and glass. Seek knowledge even unto China. Was this why...?

He was shaken from his reveries by a choking and a cry. 'Lord, help me!' The figure of Miriam Mzamane across from him was clutching her chest and her left eye was drooping. 'Pain... help!' she cried. Sayyid had done a course at the masjid about strokes and he knew the signs. But to help her would mean...

... but to not...

He shouted out for help and then grasped her outstretched hand and cradled the head that fell towards him. He stroked the wiry hair that covered it and said softly, 'It will be alright, sister, it will be alright.'

'Stay with me, please! Help me!'

People came running, chattering in Chinese.

He held the African in his arms and softly whispered, 'I will not leave you.'

---

A week later Mohammed Sayyid bin Waqas knelt down at prayer in the Huaisheng Mosque in Guangzhou. 'God is great,' he whispered to himself as he thought about the wisdom he had been blessed to receive, even unto China.

*Written May-September 2018, as final assignment for Creative Writing MA, Smallthorne, UK*

# Alto de Perdón

"Where the way of the wind meets the way of the stars."

Hans turned around. The speaker was an elderly Asian man, Japanese or Korean perhaps, his two jet-black eyes like entries into the abyss. "That is what the words say if you translate them."

"It's beautiful," replied Hans. They both stood there, letting the wind buffet their cheeks, drinking in the glory all around them; the rolling Navarran fields, the majestic storm clouds to the south, the towering Pyrrenes beyond Pamplona, the giant turbines lining the crest of the hill admitting their faint fwap-fwap as they harvested the power of the wind and the chatter of the pilgrims below as they harvested the spiritual power of the Camino. Hans had longed to walk to Santiago for years and now that he was actually walking, he was finding it more incredible than he had ever imagined.

"This hill is called the Alto de Perdón," continued his fellow traveller. "The Hill of Forgiveness. It was said in ancient times that he who confesses his sins here is forgiven all."

Hans nodded and smiled.

"Buen Camino!" said the Asian man with a smile, using the traditional pilgrim's greeting. Have a good Camino. Hans greeted him likewise but he was already on his way.

Hans did not move though. Instead he stayed there on that wind-blessed hillside and took the advice of the ancients, confessing all the sins he could think of.

And when he moved on, his pack felt somehow lighter.

---

Hans walked alone. The previous three days he had journeyed with an Australian girl that he had met just outside St. Jean Pied de Port. The fellowship had been incredible; they had talked with an intimacy which Hans rarely managed even with his closest family and friends. There was something about being on the Way that made him open up and bare his soul for the world to see. It had been intensely liberating. But that morning she had been ill with a stomach upset and could not move. "I'll catch you up," she promised. So he continued alone, just him and the path. And whilst he missed her intensely, he also enjoyed the solitude and time to reflect.

He descended the hill and was walking through fields rich with wheat ready to be harvested. Fennel grew at the side of the Way, its yellow flowers lighting his path and its scent, like liquorice, exciting his nostrils. He stopped by a large rock and took his water bottle out of his pack for a drink. Sitting on the rock he gazed all about him, drinking in the glory of creation and his heart felt like it burst from joy at all that he had seen.

"Buen Camino!"

He looked up. It was the elderly Asian man again. He had approached from behind, Hans not noticing him, so transfixed had he been by the glory of his surroundings. "Buen Camino!" replied Hans.

They walked together.

At first the man said nothing. Hans continued to take in all that he was seeing, grateful to the core for the opportunity of being able to undertake this journey. Then, after a kilometre or so, he asked, "What is your name?"

"My name is unimportant," said the man.

"And where are you from?"

"That too does not matter."

"I love this," said Hans.

"I know."

Hans looked at him and he looked back. Hans gazed into those deep, black eyes and realised.

"Did you follow the example of the ancients on the Alto de Perdón?" asked the man.

Hans nodded.

"Then all shall be well."

---

By the side of the Way of the St. James, the pilgrim path known as the Camino which leads all the way to the apostle's tomb in Santiago de Compostela, there stands a small, metal cross. You can find it about kilometre or so west of the famous Alto de Perdón, beside a large, smooth boulder upon which many pilgrims have chosen to rest over the years. The cross is festooned by pebbles, rosaries, ribbons and other small trinkets signifying a prayer being said before it. And on the front of the cross are engraved the following words:

HANS HARRIERS

DEUTSCHLAND

1967-2018

HIS CAMINO ENDED HERE

The cross was erected by Jacky Daly, an Australian lady who had walked with Harriers for the previous few days. It was also her who found him lying there on the ground only a few minutes after he had died. She'd suffered from a mystery stomach bug that morning but then it had just as mysteriously cleared up and she was rushing to catch up with her fellow pilgrim.

The coroner declared the cause of death to be a heart attack.

All she remembered was the serene smile upon his lips.

The cross was erected when she walked the Way for a second time in his memory.

*Written 14th September, 2018, Stoke-on-Trent – Liverpool Lime Street, UK*

# Lost & Found

## [1]

"James! James! Where are you! Jaaaaames!"

I cried frantically, my heart pounding, worry and worst fears streaming through my brain. My child, our child; where had he got to? "James! Jaaaaames!"

Only the forest replied.

"Don't worry, darling, he will be fine."

"How can you say that? He could have fallen? Someone could have taken him? How could he have wandered off like that? Jaaaaames!"

"We'll get the police. There's no mobile signal here but we can go back to Puente la Reina. There will be a police station there I'm sure. They can help. They have dogs and helicopters. A local may have even taken him there already."

"But we can't leave here, he could be…"

"He's ok, I'm sure. Come on. Let's go to the police; they will help us…"

"How can you be so calm. The man is meant to be the calm one and the woman the one going crazy. It's as if we've swapped roles. James could be…"

"The police, we must go to the police!"

The forest was quiet. Not a bird could be heard, not a breath of wind stirred the leaves on the branches. Only the crunch, crunch, crunch of my steps on the path and the regular inhale exhale of my breath.

Then I heard a noise. A crunch of twigs, branches brushes aside and, there before me, stood a child. He was around eight years old, with brown hair and blue eyes. I smiled at him and said, "Hola!"

"Hola!" he replied. I looked around. He was alone, and the map said that there was no settlement nearby. A child that age should not be alone. He could be in danger. The next passing pilgrim may not be as harmless as me. I summoned up my pidgin Spanish.

"Donde est tu mama?"

He looked at me blankly.

"Que es tu llamo?"

Those eyes stared back. Perhaps he wasn't local? I tried English.

"Where is your mum?"

He smiled and replied in slightly-accented but good English. "I don't know. She was here but now she is gone. I looked in the woods for her but I can't find her."

"Come with me. I will help you find her. At the next town we can call the police."

He looked unsure, perhaps mindful of school lessons warning against strangers. "Are you a peregrino?"

I smiled. "Yes, yes I am. My name is Marijke. What is yours?"

---

We walked together along the Camino, two pilgrims, young and old. I told him that I was from the Netherlands and, to my surprise and delight, he said that his mum was Dutch too. "She is from there and we go back on holiday sometime, but we live in Denmark because that is where my dad is from." He paused and looked up at me. "You remind me of my mum a bit," he said. I felt warm inside. I'd never wanted kids, or at least, not for another ten years or so, but it was still nice to hear. Some primeval maternal instinct in me stirred.

We spoke in English because his Dutch was minimal; both parents talked to each other in English and so he'd picked it up well. I was glad of all those lessons I'd had at school. We talked about his family. He told me that his sister was only three and that she annoyed him. "She cries all the time and tells tales on me and wants my mum to be with her and not me." He looked sad and started to sniffle, so I stopped, put my arm around him and explained that little kids do that sometime. "Your sister's not being nasty, it's just that she doesn't understand the world as much as you do. She needs her mum a lot as she is only a toddler really and so cannot do much by herself. But you are a big boy now; you may want your mum, but you don't need her as much. In fact, you can look after her and your sister." With those words he stopped sniffling and hugged me back. "You're great, Marijke!" he said, and I almost exploded. I'd never felt so good about anything, not even when I passed an exam or fell in love with a boy.

We left the forest and walked through fields. I showed him the different flowers, how this one smelt of liquorice and that one had berries which you could eat. We picked the berries and ate some, although he got most of them smeared all over his face. He grinned at the end and I laughed. Then he told me about the school that he went to and which cartoons he liked. I hadn't heard of any of them. It was an isolated section of the Way and we were the only ones there. Strange as this may sound, but we formed a connection, James and I, a connection that crossed the years and the nations. I started to sing a song, a silly one that we'd learned in school when we were just kids, all about London

Bridge. But he knew it and we sung along together, laughing as we went.

And as we walked and laughed, it seemed as if the fields and trees and flowers themselves were laughing with us.

After a few kilometres, we came to the village of Mañeru. We had both seen it well before: a nest of ancient dwellings crowded onto a hilltop around an old stone church. In the centre was a café. I bought him a Coke while I had a coffee. Whilst ordering, I asked the proprietor about the police. He made a call, and, after our second coffee, they arrived.

One of the officers spoke some English. She understood that he was lost, and I showed her on my map where it had happened. Then they took him into their care. He started to cry when I told him that he must go with them. He gave me a big hug and did not want to let go. I started crying too. "You'd make a great mum!" he said. I wanted to tell him that that was not in my life plan, but instead the warm feeling that his words gave me filled me up inside and so I just thanked him. He waved as the police car drove off and I waved back, both of us still crying.

And the proprietor of the café told me the drinks were on the house because I had done such a good deed.

---

I continued to walk but felt terribly alone. I missed little James with his cheeky smile and zest for life. The words he'd said to me stuck in my mind. I'd make a great mum. I passed a gate upon which someone had written 'Camino is the teacher'. Had James taught me something?

I sat down under a tree to think about it, closing my eyes in prayer to a God that I was far from sure I believed in. No answer came as I knew it would not. Sometimes the Camino gets you like that. It makes you all spiritual and you start believing everything is a coincidence or some sort of profound lesson in life. I opened my eyes and saw another pilgrim approaching, pack on his back, staff in his hand. "Buen Camino!" I greeted him. He greeted me back and I walked with him.

He was neither profound nor a teacher. But he was zany, funny and quite cute. His name was Jens and he was from Aalborg. We walked together from then on but I never forgot James.

# [3]

It was a strange trip, that summer. My wife and I decided to go back to the Camino to celebrate it being ten years since we met each other. We couldn't walk it this time of course, not with an eight-year old and a three-year old at our side, so instead we drove down in the car and stopped off at all the places that we'd remembered. For some reason Marijke wanted to stop off in the wood just before Mañeru and while we were there, James disappeared. I was frantic with worry but, surprisingly for her, she was extremely calm, serene almost. She simply told me to go to the police in Puente la Reina. We did that and, lo and behold, there was James waiting for us. He told us that he'd met a pilgrim who came from the Netherlands just like mummy and had walked with him to a village where she'd bought him a Coke and then the police had come. We both hugged him and hugged him; I had never felt worry like that in my life. I suggested we seek out this pilgrim and thank her, maybe give her some money or something, but she hadn't left a name with the police and Marijke didn't seem to want to bother. "She's had her reward," was all she said. What a queer comment. How would she know?

We stayed in Puente la Reina that night and then we pressed on. The following morning we stopped off by the Way and found the tree where Marijke had been resting when I came along. "This is where mummy and daddy first met each other ten years ago," I told James and Maria. We took out a shell, wrote 'Jens & Marijke' on it and then underneath the date that we met.

And afterwards we took a photo of the four of us, safe and sound, by that tree on the Camino.

*Written 12/10/2018, Smallthorne, UK*

# Callous Caller on the 08:25

It was her loudness that first attracted his attention. Her broad north Midlands accent which betrayed which station she had boarded at filled the entire carriage. Deprived of the choice of whether to listen to her conversation or not, he decided to enter in.

'They will just have to accept it and that is that! We are running a business, not a social service for the locals," she told the person on the end of the phone. 'Yes, I know it won't go down well, but these are necessary measures. Profits were down from those stores last quarter as you know, particularly Oldham. Quite how that branch is even staying open I don't know. She's shit, that's all there is to it. 56% below projected. Unacceptable, simple as... yes, I know it's just before Christmas but if it wasn't then it would be just before the summer holidays or Easter or Eid or something else...'

She went on. He wondered what she looked like, this callous caller on the 08:25, but she was facing away from him on the opposite table, so all he could see was the back of her head, blonde hair scraped back in a tight ponytail, and half a business suit. He wondered casually which company it was that she worked for and what they would think about her broadcasting their sales figures all over Coach C of the morning express from Euston, but then returned to his own business and the difficult meeting he himself had to deal with.

She finished off, as loudly as she had begun, making any concentration impossible. 'Yeah, we're not far off Piccadilly now. I'll take a cab, ETA 09:30. See you then.'

'Thank God', he thought, relieved that he could now attend to the Salford situation. However, he had underestimated her. 'Hi mum, yeah, it's me. Can you do me a favour? Yeah, it's the nursery. Fucking shit as always. Apparently Sienna has filled her nappy again, twice in half an hour.

They're saying she's ill and want me to take her, but I've got this meeting in Manchester. And they told me they'd be charging for the nappy. I told them that if they even tried I'd be having a bloody work with the manager. Incompetent the lot of them, fucking disgrace! Anyway, yeah, if you could have her, ta for that, yeah...'

He tried to think positively of her as Sarah would do. She would explain that the pressures of being a working mum were huge and that there is a story behind everyone. But he couldn't see it. This woman just seemed like a total bitch, pure and simple. Again, for no particular reason, he wondered what she looked like. He glanced at his mobile. Twenty-five minutes to go. Yeah, he had time for a cup of tea.

He walked along to Coach B, handed the £2.20 over and then returned holding the cup. Now he was facing in the other direction so he could check her out easily without it being too obvious. He was surprised. She was attractive; her features were pretty, sexy even. And yet, at the same time, her face had a certain harshness. It betrayed a cruelty. Then, in an instant, it happened.

It was like in one of those films where time stops still, the world freezes but the main character remains in motion. Looking at that face he saw it regress over the years. He saw the cruelty and callousness slowly disappear and in their place the innocent, fresh visage of a schoolgirl, nervous but eager to take on the world. They talk of nature versus nurture and, in that instant, he realised which of the two was to blame.

Time resumed, and he passed on by. She never noticed a thing as she was engrossed in playing on her phone.

---

He finished his tea and glanced out of the window. They were pulling into Piccadilly now. He smiled. Becky would be there to meet him on the platform and after the stormy Manchester meeting they would be going out for a meal in Chinatown and then retiring to the Midland booked on company expenses. Sarah would never know, it would be perfect. A shadow passed his mind. Was his tie straight. Did he look the part?

He got up and walked down the aisle to the toilet. As he did he turned his head to catch one final glimpse of the once-blessed now-cursed face of sick Sienna's mum. As he did, their eyes met. He smiled, and she smiled back.

In the toilet he locked the door and then turned to look in the mirror. As he did he gasped in shock. Staring back at him was a face, like the one in the carriage, once innocent and handsome, now stained with harshness and cruelty.

When had that happened? How had that change taken place? He trembled at what it meant, at what he had become.

Composing himself, he straightened his tie and went out to meet the world.

*Written on the 08:25 Stoke-on-Trent – Manchester Piccadilly,
10/12/18
Inspired by the same journey on 30/11/18*

# Did you enjoy this book?

If so, Matt Pointon has written lots more.
Check them all out and order some today
from
http://www.lulu.com/spotlight/mattpointon

# Other titles by Matt Pointon:

## Fiction

### Short Story Collections
Short Stories Volume 1: 2000-2005
Short Stories Volume 2: 2006-2010
Short Stories Volume 3: 2011-2014
Short Stories Volume 4: 2015-2016

### The Onogurian Three Chronicles
The Lost Treasure of Onoguria
The Bukhara Affair
The Revenge of the Sultan
Into the Belly of the Beast
The Bell of the North
How It All Began

### Other Novels
The Line
Tatyana Delcheva
Disco 2005

### Children's Fiction
Peril in the Peak District
Bathtime in Budapest

## Non-Fiction

### Travel Writing
The Streets Might Not Be Paved with Gold, but the Hills Are Made of Chocolate: A Trip to Hong Kong and the Philippines
Two Weeks with Uncle Ho, Brother Number One and Ming the Merciless
Dirty Magazine: A trip to Seoul and Indonesia
Across Asia with a Lowlander
Albanian Excursions
Holy Land
From the Caucasus to the Bosphorus: More Travels along the Silk Road
Balkania: A trip across the Balkans
The Missing Link
Incredible India
Among Armenians
A470
Travels in the (other) Holy Land: Part 1
On the Other Island
Letters from a Voyage to the North
Vas Bien, Fidel
An Unconnected Place: Travels in a Country the World Wishes Did Not Exist
A Break in Byzantium
Travels in a Forgotten Country

### Spiritual
A Life of St. Bertram
A Life of St. Werburgh
A Life of St. Modwen
A Life of St. Editha
A Life of St. Guthlac

### Local History
A History of the Parish of Draycott-en-le-Moors